JIGSAW GUILT

Recent Titles by Jeffrey Ashford from Severn House

THE COST OF INNOCENCE
A DANGEROUS FRIENDSHIP
DEADLY CORRUPTION
EVIDENTIALLY GUILTY
FAIR EXCHANGE IS ROBBERY
AN HONEST BETRAYAL
ILLEGAL GUILT
JIGSAW GUILT
LOOKING-GLASS JUSTICE
MURDER WILL OUT
A TRUTHFUL INJUSTICE
A WEB OF CIRCUMSTANCES

Writing as Roderic Jeffries

AN AIR OF MURDER
DEFINITELY DECEASED
AN INSTINCTIVE SOLUTION
AN INTRIGUING MURDER
MURDER DELAYED
MURDER NEEDS IMAGINATION
SEEING IS DECEIVING
A SUNNY DISAPPEARANCE
SUN SEA AND MURDER

JIGSAW GUILT

Jeffrey Ashford

This first world edition published 2009
in Great Britain and in the USA by
SEVERN HOUSE PUBLISHERS LTD of
9–15 High Street, Sutton, Surrey, England, SM1 1DF.
Trade paperback edition published
in Great Britain and the USA 2009 by
SEVERN HOUSE PUBLISHERS LTD

British Library Cataloguing in Publication Data

Ashford, Jeffrey, 1926-
    Jigsaw Guilt.
    1. Missing persons–Investigation–Fiction. 2. Dairy
    farmers–Fiction. 3. Detective and mystery stories.
    I. Title
        823.9'14-dc22

ISBN-13: 978-0-7278-6800-8   (cased)

All Severn House titles are printed on acid-free paper.

Typeset by Palimpsest Book Production Ltd.,
Grangemouth, Stirlingshire, Scotland.
Printed and bound in Great Britain by
MPG Books Ltd., Bodmin, Cornwall.

ONE

PC Curtis watched the woman approach the counter in the front room of Carnford Divisional HQ. Middle-aged, aggressive features, well-dressed, a brooch with either fake diamonds or worth thousands.

'Are you in charge here?' she demanded.

Her accent marked her as an Australian, which explained her lack of respect for authority. 'Can I help you, madam?'

'I'm just in from Gin Gin and . . .'

There were times when one was entitled to ignore the requirement to be polite to the public. 'Then you'd best go back there and lie down a while.'

Her tone sharpened. 'Gin Gin is a town north of Brisbane.'

'I'm sorry, I thought . . . You have a problem?'

'I would not be here if not.'

'Your name, please?'

'Mrs Ross.'

'Would you like to explain what is the matter?'

'I flew over to meet an old friend. She knew when I was arriving and I was expecting to meet her at the airport. Since she was not there, I phoned her home. Her husband told me she was away, staying with friends. That was nonsense. She would not have gone anywhere when she knew I was arriving.'

'Yet it seemed she did.'

'One of us is not understanding the other. She would not leave home to stay with friends when she knew I was arriving.'

'People sometimes change their minds or there is an emergency.'

'I asked Tom, her husband, for the names of the friends with whom she was staying. He said he did not know where she had gone.'

'That's possible, I suppose.'

'Then you're very free with your suppositions.'

'Mrs Ross, there is no way in which we can help you. It is not an offence to leave home without telling your husband where you're going.'

'She and Tom are always rowing.'

'Is that of any significance?'

'I have to spell things out for you?'

'I am sorry, but . . .'

'If you still don't follow, find someone who will.'

'No one is free.'

'Free someone.'

He wanted to tell her to get lost. But in his judgement, she was not a woman who would go quietly. Should she complain about his manner, he could be considered to have been rude to a member of the public, which would result in trouble. 'Very well.' Someone else could cope with her. 'If you'll wait over there.' He pointed to the small alcove with chairs and a table, on which lay several out-of-date magazines.

As she crossed to the alcove, he turned and spoke to the woman PC in the small communications room behind. 'Keep an eye out there. She's arsenic.'

He went to the end of the counter, lifted the flap and walked across to the far doorway and along the passage to the CID general room. Only Miles was present. Still officially a PC, he was completing his vocational training before, hopefully, being accepted full time in the CID.

'You're needed in the front room, Eric.'

'What's up?' Miles looked younger than his years. Women liked his curly hair, dimpled chin and shapely mouth.

'A civilian with a problem.'

'Such as?' He had a tuneful voice.

'A Mrs Ross, from the outback or somewhere, has flown over expecting to meet an old friend. Friend's not at the airport, husband says his wife has gone to stay with friends, she asks for name and phone number of friends, he says he doesn't know. She's certain something nasty is going on.'

'Doesn't sound anything much to me.'

'No one's interested in your opinion. She reckons it's

impossible for her friend to be away, knowing she was arriving.'

'A bit far-fetched.'

'When you've been around long enough, you'll know there're those who live in a different world. Take her into an interview room, listen to what she has to say, sympathize, promise you'll do everything possible, and get rid of the silly bitch.'

'But . . .'

'You won't have any trouble with her.'

Detective Inspector Tait was late middle-aged, balding, had had to have five teeth extracted recently despite regular visits to a dentist, and had a waist that was expanding despite his wife's efforts to make him reduce his appetite for rich food. He had commenced his career with the aim of ending it in the chief constable's chair; he now accepted he would retire a detective inspector because a man needed luck as well as ability to climb the higher rungs of the promotion ladder and he was not a lucky man.

He looked up from his desk when Miles, not having knocked since the door had been open, entered the room.

'I'd like a word, sir,' Miles said.

Tait prided himself on his ability to judge a man's worth, but found Miles something of an enigma. A good worker, yet sufficiently naive to believe there was good in everyone. Would he survive the pressures of the force long enough to understand there were men and women in whom there was not one iota of morality?

Miles detailed the conversation he had had with Mrs Ross.

'Why was she so certain Mrs Harvey would not have left home to go to somewhere other than the airport?'

'They were such very close friends. That's why she's so worried something has happened to Mrs Harvey. Normally, nothing would have prevented Mrs Harvey meeting her.'

'I could suggest a dozen and one reasons why not.'

'Mrs Ross again and again made the point that the Harveys are not on the best of terms, and that she is wealthy and her husband often asks her for money.'

'Most marriages it's the other way round. Did you gather anything about Harvey's background?'

'He's a farmer. Before marrying, he built up a small herd of quality . . . can't remember the breed. After the marriage, with the help of his wife's money, he enlarged and improved the herd and now it's one of the top ones in the country. Friesians, that's what they are. Wins prizes at agricultural shows. Then farming ran into trouble and soon he owed his bank a load and he was asking the wife for more. She likes to live luxuriously and resented being asked to cut back on her lifestyle and told him to find a job and keep her instead of her keeping him. Their rows became more bitter when he wanted to build a new feed barn in order to buy freshly harvested corn in bulk, and she refused to finance him and help him pay off some of his debt to the bank. He had to sell off a few of his prize cows and became very bitter towards her.'

'Mrs Ross seems to have known an unusual amount of what went on in the Harvey family.'

'The friendship between the women is obviously very close, sir. Mrs Ross often comes to England to be with her.'

'What did you make of Mrs Ross?'

'Down to earth.'

'Yet conjures up dark deeds?'

'She believes there has to be some sort of trouble.'

'Shadows darkened by imagination. What's your judgment?'

'Mrs Harvey could have been called away by a sudden emergency or she just wanted a complete break from all the rows and forgot her friend. But I don't believe that is the case.'

'Why not?'

'Mrs Ross was so insistent that whatever had happened, Mrs Harvey would have ensured they could get in touch with each other.'

'Have you considered the possibility that knowing Mrs Harvey's poor relations with her husband may be colouring her fears?'

'I'm sure that isn't so.'

'You have an infallible way of determining truth?'

Sarcastic sod, Miles thought.

'Has Mr Harvey spoken to the friends with whom his wife may be staying?'

'I can't say, sir.'

'Mrs Ross did not ask the husband whether he had contacted such friends?'

'She didn't say she had.'

'Where does Harvey live?'

'Tanton Farm in Brecton Without.'

'Without what, I wonder?'

'That's the name of the village, sir.'

Tait smiled. Miles, annoyed by his failure to realize it was a time-tarnished question, silently swore.

'Where is Mrs Ross staying?'

'Here in Carnford, at the Crown Hotel.'

'The last time I had a meal there, the crown was badly tarnished.' Tait picked up a pencil and fiddled with it. 'Go and speak to the lady. Make her understand we are doing everything possible to trace Mrs Harvey. And learn whether we need to take matters any further.'

'Yes, sir.'

Miles left. He was surprised to have been given the task. It might be a compliment. But then, of course, it might be no more than an indication that the detective inspector had decided there was no case for a meaningful enquiry.

The Crown Hotel did not acknowledge time. The public rooms remained bereft of style, grace or comfort, the bedrooms lacked space and only two had en suite bathrooms. However, the management were up-to-date with regard to the charges.

Miles met Fiona Ross in the otherwise deserted lounge, which had considerable need for redecoration. She vaguely reminded him of Aunt Dorothea, who had defied an overbearing father and reduced her mother to tears when she married a man from Paraguay. Similar sharp features, overdeveloped nose, graceful neck, careless disregard for fashion.

'I thought I had been forgotten!' was her greeting.

'Very far from it, Mrs Ross. But we have so much work in hand . . .'

'Forget the official crap. Have you learned where Gillian is?'

'I am afraid not, which is why I am here to learn if you can give us any more help.'

'I've said all there is to say, but officialdom never listens, so I'll say it all again after you've sat.'

He settled on a chair with scuffed leather and a probing spring in the seat.

'Are you a drinking man?'

'I sometimes have something when I return home in the evening,' he replied carefully.

There was a bell on the table and she rang it.

A waitress came through a doorway and up to their table. 'Hullo, Mrs Ross. Have you had any news?'

'Not yet, Daisy, but where there's silence, there's hope. We'll have something to drink. Mine's a daiquiri. George has shown you how to make it?'

'Yes, Mrs Ross.

She turned to Miles. 'And you?'

'May I have a lager?'

The waitress left.

'Nice girl,' Fiona observed. 'Can't do too much for one.'

Because she's well-tipped or responding to the unusual friendliness? he wondered. 'If I may ask you some questions?'

'Isn't that why you're here? Or is it your job to keep that fool woman quiet?'

'No one would ever say anything like that.'

She smiled; her features lost their hint of hardness. 'No offence, but you're a poor liar. All right, I could be seeing termite hills where the land's flat. But when one knows someone as closely as I know Gillian, one can be certain of some things. If she couldn't be at the airport, she'd have made certain we were in touch with each other at the first opportunity. That meant her being at home when I arrived or making certain I knew how to get in touch with her.

So when she's not at home and Harvey says he can't tell me where she's gone, something has to be wrong.'

'There could have been an emergency . . .'

'If the earth had opened up, she'd still have left word.'

The waitress brought them the drinks on a tarnished tray. She put a glass down in front of Fiona. 'I hope you'll find that is as you like it, Mrs Ross.'

Fiona raised the glass and briefly drank. 'My favourite barman back home couldn't do better.'

The waitress left.

Fiona put the glass down. 'Let's get a bit of a move on. This room makes me feel mournful.'

Miles doubted she ever felt truly mournful – there was too much life in her – but the room certainly was uncongenial.

'If I'd known there was a good hotel just outside the town, I'd have booked in there.' She drank. 'But having said I'm here, I'll have to stay, at least for a while.'

'Have you met Mr Harvey?'

'Not this trip. Just spoken over the phone.'

'What about the other times you've been here?'

'We've met.'

'Do you get on well with him?'

'I don't like cows.'

'Does that mean . . .?'

'That I don't like cows.'

'Did he explain why he couldn't say where Mrs Harvey is?'

'Simply said he didn't know. I told him that was ridiculous.'

'D'you think he was worried?'

'Impossible to tell.'

'From what you've said, he's a bit of a fanatic when it comes to his cows.'

'Gillian once suggested that if he had to choose between her and them, he'd choose the cows.'

'Was she speaking jokingly?'

'No.'

'When was this?'

'Some time back.'

'Before he was faced with the possibility of having to sell a cow or two to keep the bank quiet?'

'Before or after, I can't say which.'

'Did she ever suggest she might be thinking of leaving him?'

'She rang up in a very emotional state and said she was doing so. That's why I flew over to help.'

'If the marriage had been rocky for a time, what finally caused her to leave?'

'She'd learned about the other sheila.'

'He was having an affair?'

'So Gillian said.'

'Do you know with whom?'

'She never named her.'

'No mention of where this woman lived?'

She picked up her glass and drank. 'I'm wrong. She did say a name. What the hell was it?'

He waited.

'Helen. Likely he saw Paris when he looked in the mirror.'

'But no surname?'

'No.'

'Had he ever offered his wife violence?'

'She never said so.'

'Then you'd say he hadn't?'

'Why should I?'

'Since you're obviously on intimate terms with . . .'

'Watch your language.'

'I meant . . . I wasn't . . . I just thought that since you were on such friendly terms, she would have told you had he ever been violent.'

'She'd have seen that as so humiliating, she wasn't going to tell anyone, not even me.'

'Yet she told you he was having an affair.'

'You'd need to be a woman to understand.'

'You asked Mr Harvey to name friends with whom she might be staying and he said he couldn't. You accepted that?'

'Told him he was a bloody liar and that if he didn't give me some straight answers, I was going to the police.'

'How did he react?'

'Put the phone down.'

'And so you think . . .'

She interrupted him. 'So I know that since she didn't leave a message for me, it's because she couldn't. That bastard has murdered her.'

TWO

Tait leaned back in his chair and stared at Miles, who stood in front of the desk. 'What's she say?'

'She's convinced Mr Harvey has murdered his wife, sir.'

'You knew as much before you left here.'

Something had annoyed the detective inspector and he liked to share his annoyances. 'I thought she hadn't actually put the accusation into words until then.'

'Why is she so certain?'

'Because it could only be something very serious to prevent Mrs Harvey meeting her at the airport, staying at home, or leaving a message of where she would be.'

'Why not a bad memory?'

'I don't think so.'

'I'm interested in facts, not thoughts.'

'Mrs Ross flew over because Mrs Harvey was in a very emotional state.'

'Good background to a bad memory.'

'Mrs Harvey had said her husband was having an affair.'

Tait's voice sharpened. 'Was the woman named?'

'Mrs Ross was only told the Christian name. Helen.'

'Did she learn anything fresh about the relationship between the Harveys?'

'There were frequent rows over money. Mrs Harvey had said that if her husband had to choose between her and the cows, he'd choose the cows.'

'Any violence?'

'She never mentioned her husband had offered any.'

Tait began to tap on the desk with the fingers of his right hand. 'A man in considerable debt married to a rich woman; she refuses to give him money to help his beloved cows; she learns he's having an affair and says she's leaving him; he sees his future disappearing down the plug hole unless . . . Mrs Ross may not be as stupidly imaginative as we've believed . Harvey must supply the names and addresses of her friends. Tell Dowling to organize that. And you can go along with him.'

Miles resentfully accepted that as a vote of no-confidence. He could question Mrs Ross when she was merely a nuisance. Now that there was at least the possibility of murder, he was not up to the job.

Miles met Dowling in the yard where the CID car was parked.

'I'll drive since you haven't brought your L-plates along,' Dowling said.

Miles offered a crude comment. Peter Dowling had a rough and careless sense of humour, yet was good company. A large man, he played rugger, cricket and tennis, was a member of a gymnasium where he lifted weights, ran on a treadmill, rowed and pumped. So fit he'd be dead by forty was the general verdict.

They drove out of the yard and on to the ring road, then the motorway, until they turned off on to country lanes to Brecton Without, a hamlet of two bungalows, three houses – one of which had been a general store years before – and a public house which had managed to remain open and was noted for the real ale it served.

Dowling braked to a halt at the crossroads. 'Which way?'

'Left, right or straight ahead.'

'You're only amusing when you're not trying to be funny. Didn't you make certain where the farm was before we left?'

'Seems you didn't either.'

'Nip in to the pub and ask where it is.'

The barman said Tanton Farm was along the first road to the right and past the old apple orchard. He silently expressed his annoyance when Miles didn't order a drink in return for the information.

They passed the orchard, neglected and unproductive, a

ten-acre field in which wheat was being harvested by combine, and a herd of Friesians strip-grazing a large field down to grass.

The farmhouse was large, unremarkable in appearance and of indeterminate age, brick on top of a ragstone base, set a hundred yards back from the road. Beyond it, to the left, was a U-shaped complex of brick-built buildings, reached by a gravel drive wide enough to allow passage of a milk tanker.

Dowling braked to a halt, extracted the keys and reached for the door handle. 'There's no need for you to say anything unless I give the nod.'

'I mustn't show manners and say good afternoon?' Miles asked sweetly.

They left the car and walked the short distance to a thorn hedge. A wooden gateway gave access to the garden, which obviously received less attention than it needed, and a brick path which took them round to a pretentious portico and the front door, above which was a fanlight with leaded glass in bright colours. Dowling pressed the bell in the centre of the circular cast-iron frame on which were the words *Ducit Amor Patriae*.

'What's that mean?' Miles asked, pointing at the inscription.

'Many pretty ladies for your pleasure.'

A middle-aged woman opened the door and stared at them, with apparent disapproval. Dowling explained they wished to have a word with Mr Harvey. She directed them to the farm buildings.

As they walked along the dirt and gravel drive which ran in a slow half-circle, a concrete lorry became visible by the side of the left-hand building and started unloading to the accompaniment of a rushing noise, like a wall collapsing.

'Interesting!' Dowling remarked.

They entered the first building and to their right was an open doorway through which one end of the milking parlour was visible. They continued on into this. A row of ten milking stalls was on either side of the pit and in this a man, wearing a plastic mackintosh, was using an injector sterilizer to clean the cups of one of the clusters.

'Mr Harvey?' Dowling asked.

'Yes?'

'Can we have a word?'

'I'm not buying.'

'We're not selling. County CID.'

Harvey hung the cluster on a rail and moved along the pit to the next one. 'What's the problem?'

'We'll explain when you've finished.'

'That'll be a time yet.'

'Then perhaps you can break off for a short while?'

Harvey's answer was to lift the next cluster off its hook and begin to wash it.

'It'll help everyone if you do as we suggest, Mr Harvey.'

He finished cleaning the cluster, walked to the end of the pit, climbed the steps and released the cows, which clattered through an open doorway.

'I've little time to waste,' Harvey said.

Early forties, thick black hair, high forehead, solid features, stubborn and quick to become aggressive, Dowling judged. 'Perhaps we can go somewhere to talk?'

'There are some bales in the shed.'

It seemed the house was out of bounds.

They left the milk parlour and followed Harvey into the end of another building, which was half-filled with the more traditionally sized bales capable of being lifted by a man. He pulled three bales down from the contrived ledge halfway up the face of the stand.

'You'll know why we're here,' Dowling said, as he sat on a bale.

'Then I know a sight more than I'm conscious of doing,' Harvey replied.

'Mrs Ross, a great friend of your wife, has just flown in from Australia, expecting to meet your wife at the airport. Mrs Ross phoned you to say she had not been there and to find out if something was wrong. You told her that you did not know where your wife was.'

'Really.'

'That seems rather odd.'

'Why?'

'Wives normally tell their husbands where they're going.'

'She didn't.'

'Mrs Ross then asked you to give her the names of friends with whom she might be staying. You refused to do so. Why?'

'I'd too much to do.'

'Too much even to help your wife's great friend?'

'Yes.'

'Were you worried that you didn't know where your wife was?'

'No.'

'Most husbands would be.'

'So?'

'It might suggest that your relationship with your wife is not of the strongest.'

'I suggest that's none of your business.'

'I gather you've spent many years breeding prize Friesians?'

'Yes.'

'Is it an expensive hobby?'

Harvey's annoyance was immediate. 'Hobby? Working all hours, milking seven days a week because our return on milk is too cheap to be able to hire a good cowman, carrying and stacking after dark, coping with all the vagaries of a government that hates the countryside is a mere goddamn hobby?'

'From a purely commercial point of view, is it more profitable to keep a non-pedigree herd than a pedigree one?'

'What do you know about dairy farming?'

'Nothing.'

'Then leave things to those who do.'

'You can't give me a short answer?'

'No.'

'It sounds as if milk farming isn't very profitable.'

'It isn't.'

'Then it must help that, as we have been told, your wife is wealthy.'

'What the hell has any of this got to do with you?'

'That's what we're trying to find out. Hopefully, it will prove to be nothing and we'll be able to move on. Has your wife been helping you financially?'

'No.'

'She doesn't meet household expenses and things like that?'

After a pause, Harvey said, 'Sometimes.'

'Recently, did you ask her to help pay off your debts and fund the building of a feed barn?'

'What if I did?'

'Did she refuse?'

'Is it that damned woman from Australia who's been shooting her mouth off?'

'Because of your wife's refusal to help, you had to sell a cow or two to find enough money to keep the bank happy for a while. That must have been very unwelcome?'

Harvey did not comment.

'What is happening outside?'

The abrupt change of subject momentarily confused Harvey. 'What d'you mean?'

'A concrete lorry has been discharging its load.'

'Well?'

'What is being built?'

'Foundations.'

'For a feed barn?'

'Eventually.'

'Why not now?'

'The base will provide storage space for bulk corn under heavy plastic sheeting.'

'That's preferable to a barn?'

'No.'

'When did the work start?'

'A day or two back.'

'That's when they dug out the ground?'

'Did that myself.'

'How?'

'You'll no doubt be surprised to learn it was with a tractor and bucket.'

'Are the foundations going to cost a packet?'

'The only things that're cheap today are questions.'

'Then before your wife left, she finally agreed to give you the necessary money to have the work done?'

'No.'

'How can you afford the job?'

'I borrowed the money.'

'From the bank?'

'From a friend who knew I was in trouble.'

'His name?'

'The loan is between him and me.'

'Only if you don't want us to start having nasty thoughts.'

'About what?'

'The timing. You wanted a barn, but needed the money to build it. Your wife refused to give you any. When she learned you're enjoying yourself in another woman's knickers . . .'

'You're talking stupidity.'

'Your wife was lying when she told Mrs Ross you'd found yourself another woman?'

'Yes.'

'Seems unlikely.'

'The Australian bitch was making it up.'

'Yet it would explain why your wife supposedly left here in such a rush.'

'Why "supposedly"?'

'Because after she disappeared, you began work on the concrete foundation.'

'Are you trying to accuse me of something?'

'Just wondering aloud how you could start building work which you could not afford.'

'Maybe you didn't hear me say I borrowed the money.'

'But refuse to give the name of the lender.'

'I explained why.'

'Where has your wife gone?'

'I do not know. I keep saying that she refused to tell me.'

'Did she take a lot of luggage?'

'A couple of suitcases.'

'She left in her own car?'

'Yes.'

'You expect she is staying with friends?'

'I don't expect anything.'

'Do you have the names and phone numbers of her friends?'

'Why d'you want to know?'

'To suggest with whom she is most likely to be staying.'

'Are you inferring you don't believe she is with friends?'

'When something is suggested, we're happy to prove any inference is nonsense.'

Harvey stood, brushed off stray pieces of hay and walked to the doorway. They followed him. On reaching the house and in a gesture of inhospitality, he went inside first. The kitchen was fully equipped and the Aga was a double one. Beyond, and halfway along a passage, was a green baize covered door.

'Them and us,' Dowling remarked as he walked past.

It took a moment for Miles to understand the reference, since life below stairs had become history.

Beyond the door, the passage widened. They entered the hall and Harvey crossed to a corner cupboard on top of which was a phone and two small notebooks with indented alphabetical tags. He handed them one book. 'That's my wife's. I've no idea which is the most likely friend since I hardly know some of them.'

Dowling put the book in his coat pocket.

'My wife will need that when she returns.'

'You'll have it back before then.'

After thanking Harvey for his help – thanks which were plainly scorned – Dowling and Miles returned to their car and drove off. As they approached the village crossroads, Dowling braked to a halt. 'Half a pint of the best will go down a treat.'

'Drinking whilst on duty?'

'The urgent duty is to help keep pubs in the countryside profitable.' He switched off the engine. 'Come and find out what *real* real ale tastes like.'

THREE

The nature programme ended. Diana Tait looked across at her mother and father, who sat on the settee and were holding hands. She was part amused, part embarrassed by this open display of affection from her "elderly" parents. 'Dad.'

Tait looked away from the screen. His daughter had dressed carefully and not in the usual muddle. Meeting Jack Crampton?

'When are you going to decide?' she asked.

'What?'

'Whether you'll pay for me to go to France with Kit and Mary for a week?'

'When you tell me if anyone else is going.'

'Why do you want to know? Because you think that if Jack's with us, I'll spend all day as well as all night horizontal?'

'Diana,' Jill said, 'please don't talk like that.'

'It's what Dad was thinking.'

'My thoughts were far better occupied,' he lied.

'It's like living with a dinosaur.' She stood.

'Is someone picking you up by car?' he asked.

'Yes.'

'And bringing you back?'

'No. I'll walk in the hopes of being raped.'

Jill sighed. 'Must you? Don't be too late.'

'Nine o'clock or you'll read me a long lecture?'

'Try not to be so aggressive. I'm only thinking that you have that big party tomorrow evening and don't want to be too tired to enjoy it.'

'How can I enjoy it when I'll know Dad is wondering if I'll keep my legs crossed,' she snapped.

A car hooted once. She hurried out of the sitting room. They heard the front door being slammed shut, then the sound of a car driving away.

'Why the hell does she talk like that?' Tait muttered as he released Jill's hand and stood.

'Because she knows it annoys you.'

'Doesn't it upset you?'

'Not when it's put on and I can trust her to behave sensibly.'

'I need a drink.'

'It's a bit early. What's the rush? Annoyance at your daughter – or has work been tougher than usual?'

'I have to tell the chief super that we may have a serious case on our hands, but just perhaps, we may not. In that snide way of his, he'll tell me I can consider myself fortunate that there's not a third possibility.'

'He's always sniping at you, isn't he?'

'How can he show his authority without trying to push me around?'

'"Drest in a little brief authority."'

'When you have a teenage daughter, you don't have any authority.'

'You are going to give her the money, aren't you? She's so eager to go.'

'If Jack is joining in . . .'

'It won't provide opportunities he hasn't already enjoyed if allowed to do so.'

'You can calmly accept she's . . .' He stopped.

'Do you remember my twentieth birthday?'

'No.'

'Then you damned well should do. You took me to that expensive restaurant and we had champagne cocktails and a bottle of wine. My parents were away, so there was no one else in the house when we returned home.'

'That was different.'

'I doubt it.'

Dowling, seated at the small table in the kitchen, watched his wife as she stood by the gas stove and prepared supper. 'Did I tell you about this morning?'

'No.' Laura used a knife to check if the potatoes in the saucepan were cooked.

'We had a woman come in to the front room who got right up Alf's nose.'

'That's easily done.'

'True. Anyway, this woman came in and said there was a problem. From what she told him, Alf said he didn't think there was, so she demanded to speak to someone in charge who might have sufficient intelligence to understand what she was saying.'

Laura laughed. 'I'd liked to have seen that.'

'No more than I.'

'What was the problem?'

'She'd flown in from Australia to meet a friend who was supposed to meet her, but didn't.'

'Why bother you lot? You're not a lost persons' department.'

'She's convinced her friend has been murdered and it was her husband who murdered her.'

'You sound doubtful.'

'There's no certainty the wife hasn't just quit home. Probably to join up with her boyfriend, as he's found himself a girlfriend. A modern marriage!'

'Why say that?'

'Because it's become rare to find a couple who stay together, and if one does, one wonders why.'

'Carry on like that, and I'll start wondering why.'

Miles came to a stop in front of the illuminated show window of the estate agents, one of three in Carnford to survive the housing downturn. 'Let's buy that one.' He pointed with his right hand to one of the many photographs of houses for sale; his left arm was around her waist.

She moved closer to the window in order to see more clearly. 'Five bedrooms. That's one for us, two for the children and two for guests.'

'You're going to have a pigeon pair?'

'We are.'

He raised his hand a little, she lowered it.

'Where are the hundreds of thousands of pounds going to come from?' she asked.

'The loose change from my lottery win.'

'Your win seems to have become lost.'

'Hope springs eternal.'

'And so becomes eternally boring. Standing here, it's rather sad to know we'll never be able to live in such a lovely place.'

'Maybe . . .' He stopped abruptly.

She reached up to squeeze his hand, to show she was sorry if she'd sounded a little sharp. 'Let's move on. Mum said supper will be at eight sharp.'

They walked down the slightly sloping pavement towards crossroads controlled by traffic lights. Within fifty yards, she stopped in front of a shop selling white goods. 'Dad's said they'll give us a washing machine and wants to know what make we'd like.'

'That's very kind of them.'

'I do hope we'll be able to buy ourselves a washing-up machine. I so hate standing at the sink.'

'Isn't that a woman's favourite occupation?'

'No. Kicking a smart Alec on the ankle is . . . It must be wonderful to be rich.'

'It's just as well you aren't.'

'Why say that?'

'We're dealing with a case in which a rich woman's disappeared and it's likely her husband has bumped her off for her money.'

'You're suggesting that if I were rich, you'd think about killing me for my money?'

Women seemed to take pleasure in finding a man at fault. He repeatedly assured her that even if she were worth billions, such an appalling thought would never occur to him.

FOUR

Seated behind his desk, Tait waited for Kirby to speak again over the phone. The detective chief superintendent, head of county CID, was a man of some contradictions. Solidly large, with an aggressive manner, one might expect him to express his irritation and anger with force and profanity, yet he seldom raised his voice and usually used sarcasm to make his feelings clear; for no logical reason, he distrusted men with beards, yet had grown one until a couple of years before; he had separated from his wife, yet quite often spent a weekend with her.

'It seems the only possibility you have not yet considered is that Mrs Harvey has been abducted by aliens,' Kirby said.

'The circumstances do suggest, sir, that if she has not suffered harm, her actions have been strange.'

'You find strange behaviour to be good reason for considering murder?'

'An indicator when viewed along with the surrounding circumstances. There were money problems and then she discovered he was having a relationship with another woman.'

'How would you judge Harvey?'

'I haven't yet met him.'

'Would it be an idea to do so?'

'I'm taking things quietly, as we do not yet have reason to open a full investigation. But where his cows are concerned, it seems he can be considered something of a fanatic and his wife reckoned they meant far more to him than she did; financially, she was threatening him with the loss of more of them.'

'I knew a man who collected stamps; spent all his spare time worrying about perforations, watermarks, and whatever else there is. His wife left him after he spent just short of a thousand pounds on a stamp when he'd refused to have a holiday because he couldn't afford it. He lived happily collecting until there was a fire and his stamps were destroyed. He committed suicide.'

'You are saying . . .?'

'That focussed ambition can be dangerous. What are your proposals?'

'It's a country area, so not many houses and it'll be worth talking to people to find out if they know anything helpful. We'll question Harvey again and press him to name his friend who has lent him money. If he continues to refuse to do so, we'll point out the dangers of this and explain that there does not have to be a body for a charge of murder to be brought.'

'Lack of a body makes a case more difficult to press in court.'

'This may prove to be a case in which the circumstantial evidence is sharp enough to make the lack of direct evidence of small consequence.'

'Such evidence is never that strong. Not with a silver-tongued lawyer repeatedly telling the jury that circumstances can lie, but facts can't. However, leave that hurdle until we meet it. If there is a body, where do you expect it to be?'

'There's woodland around the farm, the largest area of which is over two hundred acres. But burying a body in a wood, however large, seems to be doomed. We both know cases where bodies in woods have come to light against all the odds. For my money, concrete is a far better bet.'

'The new footing that's being constructed?'

'I haven't been able to collate all the facts and dates, but instead of having the ground dug out by a contractor, he was in such a hurry he did it himself. That must have taken a hell of a time, which he probably needed elsewhere.'

'It saved the cost of a contractor.'

'Was that the reason? He dug out the hole very soon before Mrs Harvey disappeared and he persuaded the builders to lay concrete immediately. Like plumbers, builders don't usually turn up until one's given up hope they ever will. Why the rush?'

'What about the identity of his new woman?'

'One of the villagers may be able to give her a surname or at least enough information for us to identify her. I'd like an order on Harvey's and his wife's bank and credit card accounts. Hers will show if she has been drawing money or he had been forging cheques, his will show if he has gained credit from elsewhere.'

'Keep me posted.'

'Yes, sir.'

Tait replaced the receiver.

Detective Constable Jenner was four months from retirement and those four could not pass quickly enough. A working life filled with other people's misfortunes – with criminals who stole and swindled, maimed and killed with no thought to their victims' feelings – made for a bitter, jaundiced view of the world. His wife had said she did not know how she would cope with his being at home all day; he would get up late, read the paper, have a beer at the local, eat an unhurried meal, have a nap, and pass the rest of the day peacefully.

He knocked on the door of Tanton Farm, turned and stared past the far buildings at a field in which was a large herd of cattle. He wondered how one could become so attached to cows as to prefer them to a wealthy wife? They were large, smelly and dangerous – years before, a woman had taken a dog into a field in which a small herd was grazing and one cow had turned on her, knocked her to the ground and trampled her.

The door was opened and he introduced himself to Mrs Spens, the Harveys' housekeeper. 'You'll know we're trying to find Mrs Harvey?'

'I'd have to be blind and deaf not to,' was her answer, spoken sharply.

'It must be very distressing for Mr Harvey.'

'You've come to say that?'

'There are a few questions to ask.'

'I suppose you'd best come in, then.'

He wondered if she disapproved of all men or only

policemen. She led the way through to the kitchen. 'D'you mind if I sit?' he asked.

'If you think you'll be here long enough.'

He moved a chair out from under the table, sat. She crossed to a cupboard and opened it. 'I've little time to talk.'

'You must be very busy?'

'Aye.'

'Then I'll be as quick as I possibly can. Did you have any idea Mrs Harvey might be leaving here?'

'No.'

'There was nothing to suggest she would be?'

'I've just said.'

'Do you know when she actually left?'

'I was away for part of the day on account of my sister who's ill.'

'Sorry to hear that.'

She put two food containers on the table.

'Was Mr Harvey very distressed after she'd left?'

'How would I tell?'

By observation, he thought. 'Perhaps he knew she was going to leave?'

'Maybe.'

'Do you know what she took with her – clothes, for instance?'

'No.'

'If you looked through her wardrobe, would you be able to say what was gone?'

'I have never looked through her wardrobe as she has not asked me to do so.'

'Would you say she has a lot of jewellery?'

'I don't concern myself with other people's fripperies.'

'So you couldn't know if she took all she possessed with her?'

'That's right.'

Questioning a native from New Guinea would be more productive, he thought. 'Have you met Mrs Ross?'

'Yes,' she answered through pursed lips.

'When was that?'

'She came here and I told her Mrs Harvey was away and I couldn't say where. She obviously thought I was lying.'

To prevent Mrs Spens' resentment growing with the memory, he thought it necessary to explain away Mrs Ross' manner. 'She would have been so disappointed because Mrs Harvey was not here.'

'Disappointment is no excuse for bad behaviour.'

'People are more direct in Australia.'

'Rude.'

He was not going to change Mrs Spens' attitude. 'Did Mrs Harvey often mention her?'

'Said a very great friend would be staying. That's all.'

'So you must have been surprised when Mrs Harvey left here before Mrs Ross arrived?'

'Don't concern myself with other people's ways.'

'Did Mr Harvey explain to her when and why his wife had left?'

'You think I listen to other people's conversations?'

'Of course not. But you might inadvertently have heard him say something about his wife. Suppose I ask if you've the slightest idea why Mrs Harvey left without a word and when her friend was coming, what would you answer?'

'That I don't concern myself with what other people do or don't do.'

'Perhaps the trouble was over Mr Harvey's girlfriend?'

She was silent.

'Do you know who she is?'

'I do not.'

'Have you ever met her?'

'Once.'

'When?'

'Can't say.'

'Tell me about it.'

'It was my day off and Mrs Harvey was in London. I was with a friend and I suddenly felt ill, so I returned to go to bed.'

'You live here?'

'Would I be going to bed here if I didn't?'

With her unfortunate appearance, probably not. 'She was here?'

'And he was in a real hurry to tell me she had asked to see his cows because she was very interested in breeding for quality. The way they looked at each other meant it wasn't cows they was interested in.' She sniffed loudly.

'Did you learn her name?'

'Helen.'

'And her surname?'

'Never mentioned it.'

'Roughly, how old was she?'

'Much the same as him.'

'I imagine she was very attractive?'

'No different from most,' she answered dismissively, 'and the scar on her cheek don't help.'

'Would you call her pleasant?'

'All nice words, but they don't mean anything from the likes of her.'

'Had she come by car?'

'No.'

'Then she'd walked?'

'His car was out in the front so likely he'd picked her up. She'd be used to being picked up.'

Miaow! 'You think she lives a long way away?'

'No.'

'Why's that?'

'There was another time.'

'Tell me about it.'

'She was in London.'

'His girl friend?'

'Mrs Harvey. The phone rang and I thought he was down in the cowshed, so I answered. A woman asked for him. She sounded like the one I'd met. I was going to tell him when he came out of the sitting room, looking like he'd fallen asleep. Does that sometimes.'

'And?'

'Went back to me work . . . Didn't mean to hear.'

'Of course you wouldn't.'

'But he was talking loud. Said he'd been held up and

would be at the cross in ten minutes. When he'd finished, he went for me and said there wasn't no need for me to answer the phone when he was in the house. Annoyed I'd answered when it was her ringing.'

'Where's the cross?'

'Can't say except I've heard talk of one around somewhere.'

'Do you imagine Mrs Harvey knew about this friendship?'

'She did later on.'

'And it caused trouble?'

'You understand I was never trying to listen, but they was always having rows.'

'Over this woman?'

'Money, then it was the woman. She shouted she wasn't having him live in her house when he was messing around with some tart and if he ever saw the woman again, she'd throw him off the farm.'

'Is the property hers, then?'

'How would I know? Only telling what she said.'

'Were you ever aware of any violence between them?'

'Never known any. And he might be no better than the next man, but I'm saying he isn't ever going to hit a woman. Fred asked me if he'd belted her because she had a bad bruise on her cheek. I told him, he'd a mind like a sewer to think that. She'd fallen over and hit her face on a chair.'

'Who's Fred?'

'Does casual labour here.'

'Where does he live?'

'At the foot of the village. There's been Wades living in that house for a hundred years, or more. He and his woman – there's few will say they're married even if she wears a ring – live like misers.'

'D'you know the name of his house?'

'Perce Hall.'

'Is he the only help?'

'There's sometimes that woman.'

'Who's she?'

'A hippy,' she answered with distaste.

'What does she do?'

'I would not want to know.'

'I meant, on the farm.'

'Works with Mr Harvey. I said to him – I had to speak my mind – I was surprised he allowed her near the farm. Told me she was worth extra gallons when she was doing the milking. Don't explain why he has her in here. Asking me to make coffee for the likes of her!'

'There's one more thing. See if you can find a photograph of Mrs Harvey for me.'

Tait picked up a pencil and made another note on a sheet of paper. He looked up. 'Check if Mrs Harvey does own the house and land. It might be in their joint names, but if it's in hers alone, she had the power to kick him out and there's a bigger motive than ever for removing her.'

'But surely he could just divorce her and claim half their joint estate?' Jenner said.

'Which could leave him with one house and no land or cows, or land, cows and no house. Identify Wade and find out what he has to say.'

'Right, Guv. Mrs Spens told me the woman's name is Helen, but she doesn't know the surname. Met her once through Harvey's bad luck. He brought her home when he thought the house was empty. I asked her if the woman was real snazzy and it seems she's nothing special.'

'Not surprising. One has to be a multimillionaire before the young and beautiful come knocking at the door.'

'Another time, the phone rang and Mrs Spens answered it. She's certain the caller was Helen. She heard Harvey say he'd be at the cross in ten minutes. As soon as the call was over, he drove off.'

'Is the cross some local monument?'

'I don't know, but Mrs Spens thought there was one somewhere around. It shouldn't be difficult to find a cross within a ten-minute drive of Brecton Without. She walked to the meeting place so she lives near there. Talk to the villagers and one of them will give her a name.'

'OK.'

Jenner crossed to the door and opened it.

'Good bit of work.'

He was surprised. Praise from the detective inspector was as rare as finding a fiver in one's pocket. He went along the corridor to the general room where Miles was working at a computer. 'Eric, get on your bike to Perce Hall in Carnford. Wade who does casual work at Tanton Farm lives there – find out if he's anything to tell us.'

'Are you sure you've got that right?'

'What's bothering the youth?'

'Seems odd for a casual worker to be living in a place called Perce Hall.'

'You reckon that if a house is called Mon Repos, a Frenchman must live in it?'

FIVE

Jenner returned from lunch in the canteen – egg, bacon, baked beans, apple pie with a scoop of ice cream and constant muttered complaints from the elder civilian worker behind the counter – and laid out an ordnance survey of the area on his desk. Estimating a ten-minute drive along country lanes, he used a drawing pin and a length of string fixed around a pencil to draw a circle which was adequate, but not of Euclidean quality. There was one cross marked and this was in the village of Revel Mead.

There had been development to the north of the village – a mixture of council and private houses – which abutted the green that had been donated to the council many years before. In the centre of the green was the Saxon Cross. That a renowned expert had held that the cross dated from the seventeenth century was ignored.

Jenner parked in front of the general store, behind a dirt-encrusted tractor. Inside, the goods on sale were as varied as possible, yet unlikely to dissuade people from making frequent trips to a supermarket in the nearby town.

He spoke to a young man in a white jacket who stood by a bread rack. 'DC Jenner, county police. I'm trying to contact someone and hope you can help me find her.'

'Been driving at thirty-one in a thirty area, has she?'

Jenner smiled, despite the frequency with which he met similar stupidity. 'Nothing serious. One of the relatives is terminally ill and wants to see his niece before he pops off. But they haven't been in contact for several years and all he knows is that she moved to this area.'

'What's her name?'

'Helen.'

'Is that all?'

'The uncle is losing his marbles and can't remember the

surname. So far, he's suggested Thorne, Baird and Whiting, amongst all the others.'

A dumpy woman walked up to the young man and asked why there was no tinned custard. He told her it was on the second shelf to the right of the deep-freeze. She said it wasn't. With an exaggerated sigh, he suggested she followed him.

Jenner looked at the bread. On one of the shelves were four baguettes in plastic covers below a notice which stated they were imported from Calais twice a week. Carol, his wife, was very fond of French bread. He would take her one back.

'As blind as a bat,' said the young man as he returned. 'The custard was exactly where I said it was. Some people are just bloody stupid as well as blind.'

And others were objectionable, Jenner thought. 'I'm hoping you'll be able to recognize the niece if I describe her.'

'Not if she don't come here.'

'You might have seen her elsewhere.'

'I suppose I could have maybe,' the young man said sourly.

Jenner decided that if he were to hold the other's interest, he would have to enlarge Helen's description. 'She's in her early thirties, attractive, and has the shape a man dreams about. One other thing, she has a scar on her cheek.'

'That sounds like Mrs Gillmore, only it can't be.'

'Why not?'

'Nothing special about her figure and not what I'd call worth the trouble.'

'Is her name Helen?'

'Can't say.'

'Would the lady in the post office know what her Christian name is?'

'Might do.'

Jenner crossed the store and waited for a customer to post a small parcel before he introduced himself through the speaking panel in the safety glass to the elderly post-mistress and explained why he was asking questions.

'So I wonder if by any chance you know if Mrs Gillmore's Christian name is Helen?'

'It is. Seen it on her letters.'

'Where does she live?'

'The next village, Armshurst.'

'Do you know the name of the house?'

'Ashby. The house used to belong to a man called Ashby. Strange, calling a house after yourself, especially if you've an odd name.'

'Like Ashby de la Zouch? Where is it?'

'Out of the village. Must get lonely for her, being on her own.'

'No husband?'

'Died some years back, soon after they were married.'

'I think it'll be worth my having a word with her to find out if she is the missing niece. Many thanks for your help.'

He left the shop, remembered he had forgotten to buy a baguette, returned and bought two – he liked them as much as Carol did. Back in the car, he opened a map of the county. Armshurst was marked in such small print it took him a moment to locate it.

Half a mile after leaving Revel Mead, the road entered a wooded area. Instinctively, he accelerated, then, calling himself a fool, he braked to the previous speed. Fifty-three years old and yet still eager to clear the woods as quickly as possible because he remained haunted by the time when, unnoticed by his parents, he had wandered away from their picnic spot, seen a squirrel on the ground and tried to chase it, and had found himself lost. Unknown horrors had closed in. His parents had found him shortly after he had begun screaming, yet the terror had become printed on his mind. Even now, he occasionally dreamt he was in a vast, endless forest, in extreme, but unknown danger . . . Carol said he thrashed around in bed like one of the Furies.

Trees gave way to fields, shadows to sunlight.

Armshurst came in sight and he stopped and asked a cyclist if he knew where the house was, and was directed

down a lane to the right. The cottage was set back twenty
yards from the road; it was stone built up to a couple of
feet above the ground, then brick, two floors high, with a
sharply pitched roof with peg-tiles. At least 150 years old,
he surmised. He walked up the short gravel path – the small
front garden suggested a keen gardener – and knocked on
the panelled front door. This was opened by a woman to
whom he identified himself. She used very little, if any,
make-up and was plainly dressed. Her scar was visible, but
not pronouncedly. Not even a Frenchman would have called
her beautiful, but he gained the impression of warmth of
character.

'What's wrong?'

She suffered the alarm which his arrival so often
caused. Had something happened to a close relative; was
she supposed to have committed some criminal act?
'Nothing to worry you, Mrs Gillmore.' Hypocrisy at its
worst. 'I'm just hoping you'll be able to answer a question or two.'

'Then you'd better come inside.'

He stepped into a triangular-shaped, beamed hall, then
the sitting room with beams low enough to make him duck
his head to pass under the central one. He sat on one of
the armchairs – more comfortable than it looked – she on
the settee.

'What do you want to know?' she asked.

He regretted the distress he was about to cause. Crime
seldom affected only the victim. 'Would you tell me if you
are friendly with Mr Harvey, who lives at Tanton Farm in
Brecton Without?'

'No.'

He noticed she had gripped her fingers tightly together.
'Are you certain you aren't?'

'I've never heard the name before.'

'Do you remember Mrs Spens?'

'No.'

She was, if anything, gripping more tightly. 'She is Mr
Harvey's housekeeper. She returned to the house one day
unexpectedly and met Mr Harvey and a young lady whom

she hadn't seen before. Mrs Spens is convinced they were very worried by her return and he hurriedly introduced his companion as merely a friend who was interested in farming.'

There was silence.

'Was that young lady you?'

'No.'

'Mrs Spens will recognize that person. If you continue to deny the fact, I shall have to ask Mrs Spens to come here and meet you.'

After a while, she said, 'If . . .' then stopped.

He waited. She was staring through the window; he was convinced she was not seeing what lay beyond.

She finally spoke. 'She'll do anything to hurt him. She'll take the farm away.'

'You mean Mrs Harvey?'

She nodded, her expression one of bitter worry.

'How long have you known Mr Harvey?'

Another pause before she answered. 'It was the county agricultural show. So muddy, my foot became stuck. He helped me free it . . .'

Her words were rambling, but she needed him to understand that the relationship was no casual dalliance, but one of deep meaning. He had restored the emotional level in life she had known before her husband had died. He had made no secret of his marriage; she had soon judged his wife contemptuous of him because he was just another farmer who couldn't make a proper income.

'Has Mr Harvey spoken to you yesterday or today?'

'No. We have to be careful in case she hears him on the phone.'

'Then you may not understand that I'm here because Mrs Harvey has disappeared and I'm hoping you'll be able to help us trace her.'

'She's left him?'

'Not exactly,' he answered, aware of her sudden hope.

'I've no idea where she is,' she said dully. 'She can't understand. She thinks his farming is nothing but his wasting his time and her money.'

'Then I imagine there were rows about that?'

'She'd row over most things because they are so completely opposite in character. If he had money, he'd share every penny of it with her. She has money and begrudges him anything.'

'There must have been trouble over building a feed barn?'

'She just would not understand that it would cost money initially, but save money in the long run.'

'There will have been times when it was very difficult for him to keep his temper.'

'When she's being awful, he says to himself, speak softly, speak remorsefully or speak silently.'

'He never expressed himself more forcefully?'

'Are you trying to suggest he might have . . . have hit her?'

'In such circumstances, some men would.'

'He could not strike a woman, whatever the provocation. Please, you have to realize that. Even if she hit him, he'd never return the blow.'

'Did he ever talk about a divorce?'

'No.'

'Not in order to marry you?'

'Does that make you think he sees me as just an extra bed warmer? Not that she's warmed his bed for a long time. Tom's someone so out-of-date that for him, marriage really is for better or for worse, for richer for poorer.'

'Then the hope must have been she would divorce him or something would happen to her.'

She said fiercely, 'What kind of something are you suggesting?'

'There are many possibilities and we have to check out each one in order to find the truth.'

'I've told you the truth, but you haven't listened. His marriage turned out to be for worse, but he had made his vow and would never break it . . . Why are you suggesting horrible things when he'd never wilfully hurt anyone?'

'I am suggesting nothing, Mrs Gillmore, but there are

circumstances surrounding Mrs Harvey's disappearance which have to be explained.'

'And if the wrong explanations damn an innocent person, you don't care?' She stood. 'Perhaps you'd like to leave.'

SIX

Jenner went into the CID general room. Miles was working at one of the computers and he turned around. 'The guv'nor's shouting for you.'

'Did he say why?'

'Just asked if you'd gone down to the sea for a swim.'

'A laugh a minute. What's Wade had to say?'

'I was about to go and talk to him, but before I could . . . By the way, the skipper's back.'

'How is he?'

'Seems normal; spent time complaining.'

'I thought he wasn't due to return to work until next week.'

'He wasn't, but wanted to return before the department collapsed through our inefficiency. If you ask me, he'd rather be here than sitting at home on his own.'

'The bitch!' Jenner said forcefully. It wasn't beyond understanding that Detective Sergeant Tyler's wife should leave him, but it was that she should do so when he was in hospital. 'Why did he stop you doing your job?'

'Said the work I'm doing now was more important.'

'Not in the guv'nor's eyes. Forget it and take off and question Wade.'

'It's already nearly six.'

'Then with luck you'll finish by midnight.'

'It'll ruin my social life.'

'Temporary DCs are not allowed social lives. Question Wade in a friendly manner and not as the omniscient inter-rogator you picture yourself to be.'

'Don't imagine anything of the sort. Frank . . .'

'What?'

'I'm not certain why Wade is important. He's a casual farm labourer, so surely won't have seen much of Harvey's missus?'

'Just because Wade isn't on kiss-cheek terms with Mrs Harvey doesn't mean he can't have gathered an impression of the relationship between husband and wife. He may have heard them having a row; Harvey may have been in a temper and mentioned his feelings too clearly when they were working together. You need to find out what Wade knew about the digging out of the earth for the feed shed and whether Wade noticed changes in the Harveys before she disappeared.'

'I'll do what I can.'

'What you'll told to do. I'll have a word with the sarge to clear you quitting this work before I report to the guv'nor.'

Outside the next room, Jenner came to a stop. How did one commiserate with a man whose wife had left him? The door was shut, so he knocked.

Tyler attracted misfortune. When young, he had broken a leg playing football in the school playground and two weeks later suffered the collapse of his parents' marriage; when adult, he had invested money inherited from his father with a life insurance company and had lost it as the firm collapsed; he'd received a serious knife wound to his left arm in the course of arresting a young thug; his wife was living with a fellow police officer from the adjoining division. He had been born on a Wednesday. As he entered, Jenner said, 'Good to see you back, sarge. How goes the belly?' He was aware that his manner probably betrayed his uneasiness.

'Not so painful as it was,' Tyler answered briefly.

'It was fortunate they caught the appendix before it burst. I gather that things then become very tricky.'

'Possibly.'

Jenner accepted that small talk was unwelcome. 'I've just had a word with Eric. Told him earlier to question Wade, who's a casual farmhand and sometimes works for Harvey, whose wife . . .'

'I've read the facts.'

'Well, when I got back just now, you'd cancelled that and given him work to do. The guv'nor wants the Harvey case sorted out yesterday, so I thought it best to tell Eric to drop your work and talk to Wade.'

'You countermanded my orders?'

'In the circumstances . . .'

'Whatever they are, you do not do that without referring to me.'

'It just seemed to me . . .'

'Is of no account. Has he left?'

'He should have done by now.'

'Then you can finish the work he was doing.'

'I have to report to the guv'nor.'

'Finish it after you've reported.'

Carol was going to have a moan if he was late home. He made his way to the DI's room.

Tait, seated behind his desk, said, 'Yes?'

'I've identified the woman who Mrs Spens saw with Harvey.'

'Well?'

No suggestion of a good job done this time; Tait had exhausted his compliments. 'Her name's Mrs Gillmore, lives just outside the village of Armshurst. Her husband's dead. She first denied knowing Harvey, finally admitted they enjoyed a close relationship. Made the point more than once that they're in love as well as lovers and they would marry if possible. But Harvey is so old-fashioned, he believes a marriage is for life and would not divorce his wife – or her money.'

'So Mrs Harvey's death fixes everything, including salving his marital conscience.' Tait began to doodle with a pencil. 'I served under a DI who was an enthusiastic archer. He used to say that motive was the gold and other facts merely the red. I'd say we have a double gold – the other woman and money.'

'Mrs Gillmore was insistent that Harvey would never offer violence to a woman, least of all to his wife.'

'Which is what you'd expect her to say.' He put the pencil down. 'What about Wade?'

'Miles is on his way to question him.'

Tait's voice sharpened. 'I understood he was to do that some time ago.'

'There's been a hiccup, sir. You know Sergeant Tyler has returned to duty?'

'Of course.'

'Miles was on his way out when Sergeant Tyler said he had to do some work for him.'

'Miles didn't explain?'

'I can't answer.'

'Needs to assert himself more.' Tait rubbed his nose. 'Have you spoken to Dowling?'

'Not since I returned.'

'He's had reports from Mrs Harvey's bank and her two card companies. There's been no movement of money since Tuesday.'

'Odd, unless she has a card on an overseas bank about which we don't know.'

'We're not going to be able to check that out, are we?' Tait looked at his watch. 'It's likely the builders will have packed up work and their office is closed . . . Do you know where that is?'

'No, sir.'

'It might have been useful to have found out. It's my guess that with the present state of the economy and of farming, they'll have wanted a deposit to cover themselves for the cost of materials. If this was paid, find out if Harvey gave cash. Also, if there was any sort of rush to get the work done. And tell them to stop pouring concrete.'

'Have I the right to do that without specific authorization?'

'Any argument and tell them a refusal could be considered to be an attempt to pervert the course of justice.'

'That seems . . .'

'. . . Very good reason not to pour any more concrete.'

It was, Jenner thought, easier to order someone to cut corners than to do so oneself.

'That's all.'

He returned to the general room and checked the work Miles had been doing and which he would now have to finish. Not as much as he had feared.

Miles walked down the path to the front door of Perce Hall. Not a mansion sporting peacocks on a vast lawn, but a bungalow and a small well-kept garden in a short row of homes. He knocked on the front door, waited, knocked again.

'Who is it?' a woman called out from inside.

'Detective Constable Miles, county police. Is Mr Wade here?'

'No.'

'Can you tell me where he is?'

The door was opened by a middle-aged woman in a wheelchair. Her first words were typical. Was something wrong? Had Fred been injured? He assured her that the only reason for his presence was that he wanted to ask her husband one or two questions.

'He said he'd be working at Ash Farm.' She had a slight defect of speech that could make her difficult to understand. 'There's a ten acre field to stook.'

'I'm an ignorant townie.' He smiled. 'What's stooking?'

'Lifting and stacking sheaves in the field to dry and ripen.'

'I didn't know anyone did that any more. Thought it was all combines.'

'The crop is for the straw, not the corn, which will be used for thatching when Norfolk reed can't be afforded. So it can't be put through a combine. Back when I could move, I regularly went stooking. Very tiring.'

'I'll bet it was.'

'But it was genuine farming.'

She always preferred the past because then she was mobile? 'Can you explain where Ash Farm is?'

'Which way is your car pointing?'

'Towards the T-junction.'

'Then turn left there and Ash Farm is a mile or so along on the right.'

Miles thanked her, returned to his car, drove past half a dozen small houses and another bungalow, and turned left at the T-junction. The farm was marked by a wooden name board. A woman in the farmhouse directed him around a field of grass ready for silaging, to a ten acre field. On part of this, stooks were lined up with military precision; on the remainder, the sheaves still lay on the stubble and four men were stooking them. He spoke to the nearest worker and was directed to Wade. Middle-aged, thick black hair speckled with chaff from the sheaves, face squarish, features unrefined, body thickset. 'Detective Constable Miles, county CID.'

Wade stared at Miles, his expression one of fear. Remembering the pheasants he had poached, out of season, the firewood illegally cut and the wandering chicken, which wandered no further? 'There's no panic, it's just a question, or two.'

'Why?'

'Because you sometimes work at Tanton Farm.'

'What if I do?'

'Then you've not heard that Mrs Harvey has disappeared?'

'No.'

'She vanished a time ago.'

'Mr Harvey never said. And what's it to do with me?'

'Nothing directly, but you must see her quite often and talk. But before we go any further, let's sit.'

'I've got to work.'

'Won't keep you for long. Not glad of a rest? Isn't it tough on the fingers?'

'What?'

'Lifting the bales by the twine.'

There was no response.

Miles sat on the stubble near the thorn hedge. After a while, reluctantly, Wade settled by his side, picked up a single stalk of wheat which had escaped from a sheave, broke off a length and began to chew this.

'Let's start with how long you've worked at Tanton Farm?'

'Since I asked him if he'd any work, couple of years back.'

'So you've seen Mrs Harvey pretty often?'

'What's it matter?'

'I can't answer that, but I'd like to know the answer.'

'Can't say.'

The traditional thick country worker? 'Do you work alongside Mr Harvey or on your own?'

'Depends on the job.'

'You help with the milking of the cows?'

'Did a couple of times, but the yield went down. Wasn't no fault of mine, but he thought it was and never told me to do it again.'

'Would you call Mr Harvey friendly?'

'As much as anyone what pays the wages.'

'When you're together, you talk about this and that?'

'Only when we don't need our breath for what we're doing.'

'What do you normally chat about?'

Wade shrugged his shoulders.

'Does he often mention Mrs Harvey?'

'No.'

'We've been told their relationship isn't of the happiest. Seems they row quite a lot.'

'Maybe.'

'You wouldn't know?'

'Don't listen to what don't concern me.'

'Very sensible. Do you know Mrs Gillmore?'

'No.'

'She's a friend of Mr Harvey. Mrs Spens has maybe mentioned her when she gives you a cup of tea and a biscuit in the middle of the morning?'

'There ain't ever a biscuit.'

'Has she mentioned Mrs Gillmore over the tea?'

'Says it's terrible he behaves like that. Gets real worked up about it and talks that the devil's winning all the time. Don't like people having a bit of fun and Mrs Gillmore must give him a lot more than his wife ever does. Like a dried-up apple, she is.'

'There's someone else works on the farm, isn't there?'

'Just him and me.'

'Mrs Spens mentioned a young woman. Called her a hippy – I thought they'd disappeared with time. You know whom I'm talking about?'

'Minnehaha.'

'Odd kind of a name.'

'That's what she's called.'

'Tell me about her.'

'Nothing to tell.'

'Where's she from?'

'Lives with a bunch of drop-outs.'

'In a commune?'

'Wouldn't know.'

'Where do they all hang out?'

Wade shrugged his shoulders.

'Can't you tell me anything about her?'

'Best ask Mr Harvey for that.'

'Why?'

'First time she showed up, I told her to clear off. He turns up, talks to her for a long time and she's helping with the cows.'

'I thought a farmer didn't like a stranger dealing with his stock?'

'Depend who's offering what.'

'How do you mean?'

'No business of mine what they do.'

'But it is of mine. You're suggesting they like each other?'

'He seems to think she's a bit of all right.'

'You don't?'

'Needs a bath and some decent clothes.'

'Decent as in smart or as in hiding what should be hidden?'

'Don't care what she shows.'

'In other words, of a generous nature. You think he's attracted?'

'When the wife's not around.'

'So he enjoys a bit of slap and tickle?'

'Something like.'

'You must have often talked to Minnehaha.'

'Says hullo and that's it. She ain't wasting time on the likes of me.'

One could hardly blame her.

Miles entered the detective sergeant's room.

Tyler had just made a mistake in drawing up a night duty rota and his expression matched his humour.

'I'm back from questioning Wade, sarge.'

'Learn anything?'

Miles gave a résumé of the meeting. 'He says Mr Harvey reckons she's really smart with the milking, or something.'

'He's suggesting hanky-panky? Is that a possible?'

'Can't judge without seeing how she wriggles.'

'You haven't spoken to her.'

'No.'

'Why not?'

'How do I get hold of her?'

'You didn't think to ask Wade?'

'He doesn't know any more than she probably lives in a commune and is called Minnehaha.'

'The world gets dafter.'

'I think the name comes from a poem written by someone.'

'Since poems don't write themselves, that's more than likely.'

'Shall I report to the guv'nor what Wade's suggesting?'

'What's his evidence?'

'He didn't quote anything specific. I expect it's the way she is with Mr Harvey. One can always tell.'

'Then why didn't Mrs Harvey know about Mrs Gillmore?'

'Can't have seen them together, looking at each other with bed in their eyes. D'you think Mr Harvey's fun with Minnehaha has something to do with Mrs Harvey's disappearance?'

'How?'

'He was scared she'd find out about that as well.'

'She'd eventually have forgiven jollies with one woman, but not with two? You've a long way to go to understand women.' There was bitterness in his voice. He had been thinking of his wife, not Gillian Harvey.

'Do I . . .'

'You'll note everything down in your workbook, then you'll find this ha-ha woman and learn the intimate details.'

'I'll get hold of her tomorrow.'

'What's stopping you moving now?'

'It's already late.'

'Where you're concerned, five in the afternoon is late for packing up work . . . All right, in the morning.'

Rumour was spreading. In the Black Swan, Mrs Harvey had had a serious accident which had left her in a coma. In the Duke of Wellington, judgment was more dire. Mrs Harvey had been murdered by her husband. The local vicar, in his vicarage, wondered whether his coming sermon should rest on the quotation, "Judge not that ye be not judged." In the end, he decided it might seem as if he were suggesting a guilty man should not be judged.

SEVEN

Tait arrived at his office, sat, yawned. Jill had suggested they taped the TV programme the previous night because it continued until midnight, but he had preferred to sit up and watch. It had proved to be thought provoking and he had not found it easy to batten down his thoughts when in bed. He had not slept well.

Tyler entered. 'Morning, sir.'

He was tempted to give the childish reply that it wasn't, but rank demanded the observation of mature decorum. 'What's the tally?'

Tyler detailed the night's crimes – drunken hooliganism, driving under the influence, car theft and joyriding – in one case of which there was a wrecked Jaguar and two youths in hospital – two break-ins, one domestic violence.

'A quiet night,' Tait said bitterly. The coming night would be busier around the pubs and clubs. It was difficult to remember that when he had joined the force, a posting to a market town had been considered an easy one.

'One more thing. The local press are below, wanting a story on Mrs Harvey.'

'I suppose we should be thankful it's taken this long to surface. The Courier or the Post?'

'Post, sir.'

'That insufferable redhead?'

'I'm afraid so.'

'Women's equality at its most pugnacious . . . Have you any indication of what line she'll be taking?'

'She's asked if we suspect violence. When I told her there was no reason to do so, she wanted to know why then were we conducting an investigation into an incident which normally would not concern us.'

'I suppose she'll misquote everything I say.'

'There's one advantage if she hots things up. If Mrs

Harvey is hiding herself away, publicity could winkle her out.'

'At my expense.'

Tyler said nothing.

'In the face of the known evidence, do you think she is alive?'

'I wouldn't bet on it.'

'And nor would I.'

The office of Anderson and Son was five miles south of Dawstone, in a Victorian house converted to commercial use. When, five years previously, Bushell had moved the business there (no Anderson was now with the firm) there had been objections on the grounds that it was a residential area. Useless objections, since Bushell's cousin was on the local council.

Jenner climbed the stone steps to the portico, entered what had been the hall, read the list of occupants in the offices, turned right and went into a room in which were filing cabinets and a desk at which a secretary worked; on her desk was a vase in which were half a dozen roses. They reminded him that it was Carol's birthday in a fortnight. Did he give her a box of the very expensive chocolates she so liked or something practical, like a new microwave oven?

'Do you want something?' the secretary asked.

Yes, the answer to my problem, he thought. 'If Mr Bushell is here, I'd like a word with him.'

'You have an appointment?'

'DC Jenner, county CID.'

She regarded him with sudden curiosity before she spoke over an internal phone. 'He'll see you now,' she said, as she replaced the receiver. She pointed. 'Over there.'

He entered a high-ceilinged room with moulded frieze. A thickset man, in his late fifties, stood near a doorway. 'Mr Bushell?'

'That's me. Come in.' Bushell moved to one side to allow him easier access, followed him inside, crossed to his desk and gestured with his hands at a comfortable chair in front of the desk, then sat.

Jenner judged Bushell to be sharp, aggressive and pig-headed. Necessary for success in the world of building.

'You've come to tell me you've finally retrieved the tiles?' Bushell demanded, his accent suggesting an East London background.

'I'm afraid not.'

'One thousand five hundred tiles from a seventeenth century house being demolished. Not far short of their worth in gold these days. The bastards scrambled over the chain link and razor wire, nicked the lot. Had the tiles ready for a roofing job out at Shorley and now I've nothing to do that with.'

'Bad luck.'

'Wouldn't be if there was more of you around in the middle of the night instead of sleeping.'

A slanderous observation often levelled at the police.

'So if it ain't them, what do you want?'

'To ask about the job at Tanton Farm.'

Bushell opened a drawer in his desk, brought out a pack of cigarettes. 'You smoke?'

'Gave it up last year.'

He tapped a cigarette out of the pack. 'The scaremongers worn you down?'

'My wife did.'

'They'll stop a man doing anything . . . Tanton Farm? Foundations for a feed barn. What about them?'

'You know Mrs Harvey seems to have disappeared?'

'Been told by enough people. And you lot are asking questions by the dozen. If you're asking me where she's gone? I don't know.'

'When were you asked to do the foundations?'

'When it was to be a feed barn. Maybe nine months ago.'

'It's taken you nine months to get started?'

'Mr Harvey saw the estimate and accused me of wanting to bankrupt him.'

'Which annoyed you so much, you've waited until now.'

'Went over my head, like always. If I worried about what people say, I'd chuck the job in and join the slackers on social security.'

'So where did you go from there?'

'Mr Harvey wanted me to give him credit and let him pay off the total in good time – said the barn would be making him extra. Had to explain I wasn't a charity and materials and my chaps have to be paid.'

'That was an end to the barn?'

'Yes.'

'But the work's started?'

'Mr Harvey came back recent and said if I'd lay just the floor, he could stack bagged corn on it, which would be covered with heavy plastic sheeting. Told him I couldn't get around to doing it until my digger was repaired, so if he was in a hurry, he'd have to have a contractor in. Told me he'd do the excavation himself. I said . . .' He stopped.

'What?'

'There was still a problem. Only he'd told me how he'd started on a shoestring, worked twenty-five hours a day, his pride when he won his first championship, how he was fulfilling his ambition . . . And that got me thinking I didn't want to be responsible for destroying all he'd worked for. Shows what a bloody fool I can be. Bring emotion into business and it's like arsenic in a cup of tea.'

'I don't follow.'

'I told him a thousand quid would cover the job if it was paid up front.'

'That was being generous?'

'Don't remind me.'

'Has he paid you?'

'Wouldn't be there if he hadn't. I may be a bloody fool, but I'm not mental.'

'When did he pay?'

'End of the week. Wanted me to start then and there. I told him, I might think of letting other clients down by doing his work first, but I wasn't having my lads lose their weekend.'

'Did he give you a cheque?'

'Cash.'

'Did it surprise you to be paid so much in notes?'

'No.'

'Funny how builders like to be paid in cash.'

'Funny how you coppers always think the worst.'

Jenner stood. 'One last thing.'

'What?'

'You're to stop the concreting.'

Bushell said violently, 'Are you round the bloody bend?'

Jenner repeated the order.

'Not sodding likely before you hand me an official order and the name of who'll be footing the bill for the wasted time.'

'I said, find where Minnehaha hangs out and question her to learn what she knows and if Harvey is fooling around with her,' Tyler said.

'Like I mentioned, it may be a job to find her, sarge,' Miles said.

'Setting things up so as you disappear for half a day and no questions asked? There won't be any difficulty if you can be bothered to use a little intelligence and ask the right questions. Get moving out to Dawstone.'

'Why?'

'Because there's said to be a commune somewhere near there. When you're finished, come straight back and report.' Tyler pointedly looked at his watch.

Miles crossed to the door.

'Any thoughts?'

'In what way, sarge?'

'What to do first?'

'When I get near Dawstone, find someone who . . .'

'You phone Tanton Farm to find out if she's there now.'

He might be inexperienced, but Miles had at least learned some of the tricks of his trade. 'I was off to do just that.'

Tyler belched.

Having determined Minnehaha was not at the farm, Miles left divisional HQ and drove towards Dawstone, either an overgrown village or a small town. When half a mile away, he saw a parked post office van and as he braked to a halt, the postman walked down the drive of a house, on to the road and around the van. 'Need help, mate?' he asked cheerfully, as he part opened the driving door of the van.

'I'm looking for a commune and I've been told there's one around here somewhere.'

'You're talking about the bunch of weirdos who call themselves born-again hippies?'

'Sounds about right.'

'Then try The Grange.'

'Where's that?'

'Through the town and out on the London road. Turn left by a signpost to Etchley and there's this old house, ready to be pulled down.'

'Thanks for the help.'

'No sweat.'

Miles drove into the town and out on the main road, then turned off this as directed. In half a mile, he came to a ponderous stone gateway, with elaborate wrought-iron gates in urgent need of repair. He turned into the weed-covered drive. On either side was a tangle of bramble, bracken, untrimmed bushes, straggling grass, one or two sad flowers, and dozens of discarded tins and bottles.

The house was a large Edwardian pile of no architectural merit, built for a financier who had wanted people to know he was wealthy. Windows were broken, their wooden frames were rotting, guttering hung down and, to the right of the portico, spray cans of different colours had been used to paint a scene which might have been of anything – or nothing. Attached to an improvised flag pole was a home-made flag; the slight breeze unfurled it sufficiently to make legible the words 'bugger off' sprayed on it. An improvised barbecue had collapsed into a jumble of bricks, grating, half burned wood and congealed, rancid fat.

The heavily studded double front door was open and one half tilted to its right so that the corner of the base was hard against the floor. He entered the large hall. One wall had been partially sprayed by someone with talent, depicting a naked woman lying on a patio chaise longue by a pool. The surface of the marble floor was badly scuffed, and battered empty lager cans and several sticks suggested games of improvised hockey were played on it.

'What d'you want?'

He looked up. The stairs had heavy, carved balusters and two of them had been tarred and feathered. At their head stood a young woman whose shirt had several buttons undone and whose shorts were ragged.

'You're trespassing.'

Her light brown hair was tangled, her earrings were an absurd size, and there was a button in her right nostril and another in her lower lip. Certainly sufficiently dirty and dishevelled to be a communard.

'Are you dumb?'

'Deaf and blind as well,' he answered.

'You're trespassing.'

'So you said.'

'Then clear off.'

'This is your house?'

'Yes.'

'Then if I were you, I'd stop throwing stones through the windows.'

'Trying to be smart?'

'Never waste my time on the impossible.'

'What are you doing here?' she demanded, annoyed by his cheerful attitude.

'I'm looking for someone.'

'Some mummy dear wants her darling back home?'

'It's not my job to collect strays.'

'Calling me a stray?'

'No. But I would like to know what name to call you.'

'Don't bother.'

'Will Mirabel be right?'

She said nothing.

'Caroline?'

She remained silent.

'Bernadette?'

'Plain Jane and you're getting on my tits. I'm going to call Bull to throw you out.'

'Horns on humans are considered to be illegal weapons.'

'You're beginning to stink of fuzz.'

'Actually, it's Chanel Number Five.'

She unexpectedly laughed, momentarily bringing youthful pleasure back to her face. 'You're a right cool bastard.'

It was a compliment. 'More DC Plod.'

'A detective?' She came down the stairs and moved towards him. 'I've always wanted to meet one socially. Know why?'

'No.'

'To see if it's twisted like the rest of you.'

'A secret.'

'Not so cool,' she said with contempt. 'So now sod off.'

'I want to have a word with a young lady who lives here.'

'If she's that, I am a bleeding duchess's daughter.'

'I don't think that would surprise me.'

'Then you're about to read me a sermon on returning to my grieving parents and making the best of the life God gave me instead of throwing it away.'

'I'm going to ask you to find Minnehaha for me.'

'Her!'

'You disapprove of her?'

'Ninety-nine pence short of a quid. Goes off to a farm and helps look after cows, so comes back stinking of shit.'

'I gather she likes cows.'

'I don't spend my time helping in stables because I like horses.'

'You once had a couple of them?'

'Sod what I once had.'

'Have you stopped to think . . .'

'No,' she answered harshly.

He knew someone more experienced than he would call him mindless for thinking he was a social worker, yet he said, 'Whatever forced you to leave home . . .'

She cursed him as a Sally Ann fool.

'Where is Minnehaha likely to be?'

'With the cows.'

'She isn't at the farm.'

She shrugged her shoulders.

'Have you seen her today?'

'How do I know?'

'By thinking.'

'About how do-gooding is all crap?'

'Have you seen her today?'

'No.'

'Will you help me find someone who'll know where she is?'

'No.'

'A little help from you will persuade me not to arrest you for local pilfering.'

She called him many names, then suddenly shouted in full voice, 'Bull', causing him to start.

'He may know where she is?'

'Maybe. They've been a shack job for a while.'

A half-dressed man, beer belly shaped by a belt around his low-slung jeans, appeared in a doorway.

'It's the fuzz,' she said.

Bull hawked and spat through a tangle of moustache and beard. 'What's he want?'

'To know where Minnehaha is,' Miles said.

'Ain't here. Hasn't been for days.' Bull returned through the doorway.

'Where d'you think she might be?' Miles asked.

'Here, there, somewhere else,' she answered.

'Perhaps she's told someone where she was going?'

'Not me.'

'What about your friend, Bull?'

'No friend since he tried to take me in my sleeping bag.'

'He could possibly know more than you do.'

'You don't understand a bloody thing. We're here because we want to be free. We don't tell where we're going, where we've been or what we're doing. She's just taken off. Fed up with being here, so going there. Maybe she'll come back, maybe she won't.'

Was there something to admire, he wondered, in people who lived outside the constrictive boundaries of the modern social state?

EIGHT

Tait dialled and after two rings, the call was answered. He asked to speak to Detective Chief Superintendent Kirby, and was told to wait. He began to tap on the desk with his fingers to the rhythm of The Blue Danube.

'Yes?'

'Inspector Tait, sir.'

'Well?'

Curt contempt for social nuances. No hullo, how are you. Time was cruel. He and Kirby had been together at the training school and assessments of their abilities had placed them as equals; yet Kirby had climbed high up the ladder and there was reason to believe he might finally make the top, yet DI Tait would always stay on the rung on which he now stood. Why the difference? Luck, the right contacts, a notable and successful case at the right moment?

'Re: the Harvey case. Efforts to find Minnehaha, the young woman who gave a voluntary hand on Tanton Farm, have failed. We have identified where she has been living, but she left there a short time back and no one knows where she's gone.'

'What were you hoping to learn from her?'

'Mainly whether she could provide any further information about the relationship between the Harveys.'

'You thought that likely?'

'Only possible, since she was in contact with Harvey with the cows. I doubt it's worth taking further time and effort to trace her.' He paused, but there was no comment. 'Bushell – the manager of the building firm, Anderson and Son – has been asked to stop concreting. He shouted, but was persuaded into falling in line.'

'You've seen the local paper?' Kirby asked.

'No, but I've been told there's a mention of the case in

it. I had a reporter here and told her we have no indication to suggest where Mrs Harvey may be.'

'You satisfied her we're treating the case as a simple missing person?'

'Yes.'

'There's not much moving in the world right now so it's possible the nationals will become interested. You still believe she is buried under the concrete?'

'Circumstances certainly suggest that, sir.'

'But don't prove it.'

'The proof will be in the results of the excavation.'

'We've no hard evidence. Should we excavate and there's no body, we'll be made to look like fools and have to bear costs we cannot afford.'

'It may all be circumstantial evidence, but she . . .'

'Good circumstantial evidence can often be torn apart by a sharp lawyer. Right now, I am not prepared to issue the order for the excavation you are requesting. If further evidence of a decisive nature turns up, I will reconsider.'

'Very well, sir.'

Tait replaced the receiver. Had he been in Kirby's position, he would have agreed to the excavation. All right, there was not one piece of circumstantial evidence which examined on its own could not be explained away, but when all were considered together, it was difficult to believe Mrs Harvey had not been murdered by her husband.

He went into the next room. Tyler was working on a computer. Time after time, politicians promised to reduce the paperwork the police had to deal with, but it only ever increased. Triffids.

'Has anyone questioned Harvey again?' Tait asked.

'Not yet, sir. We've had a couple of jobs come in that are keeping everyone busy.'

'More important than learning how Harvey raised a thousand pounds in cash?'

'It's difficult to prioritize . . .'

'I want the questions cleared up sharp.' Tait left.

Tyler was about to switch off the computer, then remembered to save. A narrow escape from the loss of two hours' work. He stood. Laugh and the world laughed with you, suffer and you suffered alone. He wondered if Tait's manner meant a bollocking from on high. He hoped so. Schadenfreude could ease one's resentment.

Dowling was in the general room.

'Where's Frank?' Tyler asked.

'On the Asda case, Sarge.'

'Have you eaten?'

'Half an hour ago.'

'What are they serving?'

'Tuna salad or shepherd's pie and treacle tart.'

'Must be somebody's birthday. Are you up to date with the Harvey case?'

'Reasonably so.'

'Find out where Harvey obtained the thousand quid to pay the builder and the identity of whoever has promised to fund the full cost of the feed barn.'

'That'll be the same person.'

'Still not learned to ask the question before you give the answer?'

'I'll work that out.'

Dowling's good humour annoyed Tyler. Back in his room, he sat and stared at the wall. How long was it now before he retired?

Dowling parked in front of the farmhouse. The wind brought the scent of cows, an unwelcome product of the country-side. He crossed to the front door, knocked. Mrs Spens opened the door. 'Is Mr Harvey around? DC Dowling, county CID.'

'Another one,' she muttered sourly.

'Depends on the classification,' he said humorously.

'You'd better come in and I'll tell him you're here. And make certain your shoes aren't covered in muck.'

As he waited in the hall, he studied the framed print of a windjammer under full sail. When young, he had known an old man who had served on a barque, one of the very few then still at sea, which sailed to Australia to load wheat. The tales of wild storms – drifting in the doldrums,

furling topgallants in a race against an oncoming squall
– had fired his imagination to the extent he had decided
to go to sea in sail despite the need to knock the weevils
out of the hard tack before eating it. The lack of any
seagoing clipper, barque, barquentine or schooner had
doomed his ambition . . .

'Good afternoon.'

He faced Harvey – someone who kept his body in trim,
he judged. He returned the greeting.

'Would you like to come in here?'

The sitting room was lived-in comfortable. A farming
magazine was on the floor, a laptop, open, was on a small
table littered with papers. They sat.

'Have you any word of where my wife is?' Harvey asked.

'I'm afraid not.'

'Why are you here, then?'

'There are one or two more questions I'd like to ask.'

'As quick as you can. I've a load of work to do.'

'We've learned the barn will not be built for the moment,
yet the concrete foundation is being laid.'

'Well?'

'Mr Bushell and you came to an agreement about the
work?'

'Wouldn't be doing it if we hadn't.'

'I meant over the cost.'

'Same answer.'

'Was this just before he began concreting?'

'Yes.'

'What were the details of the agreement? Did you have
to pay a deposit?'

'Yes.'

'How much was it?'

'A thousand pounds.'

'You paid by cheque?'

'Cash.'

'Rather a large amount to be in cash.'

'Not these days.'

'Would you mind telling me where the money came
from?'

'I would.'

'Why is that?'

'I am fed up with having my private life raked over.'

'Unfortunately, that has become necessary.'

'Has it?'

'If we are to have the best chance of finding your wife.'

'The one place you won't find her is under the concrete.'

'Has it been suggested we would?'

'You imagine I don't understand why the concreting has ceased at your orders and why you ask endless questions?'

'Will you tell me from whom you obtained the thousand pounds you paid Bushell?'

'No.'

'That does seem irrational. If there is a ready explanation, why not give it and clear the air?'

'And if I don't, I must have a criminal reason for not doing so? It doesn't matter how often I tell you I don't know where my wife is, how often I answer the same questions, your minds are fixed. You are teaching me that innocence is no match for stupidity.'

'When you were first asked about how you would pay to have the barn built, you answered a friend was lending you the money and the saving in feed costs would enable you to pay off the debt in a reasonable time.'

'So?'

'Who is your friend?'

'For the umpteenth time, I am not prepared to name him.'

'If you are in a position to have the barn built, why are you not doing that? Why confine the work to the foundations?'

'The money became less readily available than we'd both hoped.'

'You are sure your friend is not mythical? You had not hoped you would be able to persuade your wife to provide the money? She did not refuse your request and, angered by the constant need of money for the farm, said she wouldn't spend another penny on it?'

'No.'

'You faced the break-up of a lifetime's work. But when

we questioned you following her disappearance, you realized the danger to yourself if you admitted her refusal, so
you invented a rich and kind friend. Is that not the truth?'

'Where's the point in arguing?'

'You admit there never was such a friend?'

'I admit nothing. I'm saying it doesn't matter what I tell
you, you have your preconceived ideas and stick to them
even though they could not be more wrong.'

'With no benefactor, you cannot have a feed barn. So
why a foundation?'

'I've explained that God knows how many times. She is
not buried there, or anywhere.'

'Interesting you should make that denial again. In fact,
I was just checking that you wanted the base to store corn
on it until a barn was built.'

'Like hell that's all you were doing.'

'How did you afford the thousand pounds deposit you
had to pay before the work began?'

'What if I tell you a friend lent it to me?'

'I would be tempted to think you had small imagination.'

'I have more than one friend who could and would lend
me that much.'

'Then name the one who did.'

There was silence.

'Mr Harvey, I'll be frank with you. There need to be
answers to our questions. When there are none, inevitably
we believe it possible you have a black reason for remaining
silent. So if you will answer the questions, you will be
helping yourself as well as me.'

'I borrowed a thousand pounds.'

'As you wish.' Dowling said goodbye and left. Harvey's
manner confused him. The obvious thing to believe was it
had been because of guilt. He was certain there had been
guilt, yet it had not seemed to be focussed on the unspoken
accusation of murder.

Fiona Ross strode into the front room at divisional HQ. PC
Curtis turned to his companion, Cadet Trent, and told him
to man the desk before he hurriedly left.

She came to a stop by the counter. 'Where's he going?'

'I beg your pardon, madam?'

'You only understand Urdu?'

Trent, a month out of preliminary training, said uneasily, 'I'm afraid I don't follow.'

'Tell him I want to talk to him.'

'PC Curtis?'

'In here, things become as confusing as a one-dollar watch. I want to speak to Detective Inspector someone-or-other.'

'Inspector Tait?'

'Sounds about right.'

'You have an appointment?'

'You lot work to punched tapes? No, I don't have an appointment. Yes, I want to talk to Inspector Tait. Now, not tomorrow.'

'Your name, please?'

'Mrs Ross from Gin Gin. And before you try to get smart, that's a town north of Brisbane. Do I need to tell you where Brisbane is?'

'Queensland, Australia.'

'A Pommy who knows it isn't in New Zealand! You're heading for promotion.'

He was fascinated and made uneasy by her brash manner.

'You appear to have two legs, so how about using them?'

Trent hurried into the detective sergeant's room. 'There's a woman out front demanding to speak to the DI. Doesn't have an appointment and doesn't give a damn for anyone. You'd better have a word with her.'

'A local?'

'She says she's from Gin Gin in Australia.'

'My God! Mrs Ross!'

'You know her?'

'Tell the Guv'nor she's asking for him.'

'Wouldn't it be better if you . . .'

'Do as you're ordered.'

Trent went into the next room. 'Sir.'

Tait was suffering from indigestion, made more unwelcome

because his wife had warned him he would so suffer if he ate any more apple strudel. 'What the hell is it?'

'There's a lady at the front desk who wants to speak to you.'

'Tell Sergeant Tyler to deal with her.'

'But . . .'

'Are you incapable of doing as you're told?'

'Sir, Sergeant Tyler thought you should speak to her.'

'A sergeant tells an inspector what to do? Why does she want to talk to me?'

'She didn't say.'

'And you lacked the foresight to ask. Did you manage to summon sufficient initiative to find out what her name is?'

'Mrs Ross, sir.'

'From Australia?'

'Yes, sir.'

'What have I done to send me down to the seventh circle of hell?'

'What was that, sir?'

'Tell her I unfortunately collapsed ten minutes ago and am waiting for the ambulance to rush me to hospital.'

Trent turned and started to walk towards the door.

'A little savvy would be an idea. Show her in and tell Sergeant Tyler that if she's still here in ten minutes' time, to come in and say there's an emergency.'

'Do you . . .'

'Do I what?'

'Mean that, sir?'

'There are times when I become convinced that modern education does not exist. Yes, I mean that.' His stomach gurgled.

Three minutes later, Fiona Ross entered. Tait stood. She came to a stop in front of the desk. 'It's taken half the day to get this far.'

'We are very busy . . .'

'Right now, you don't look up to doing much.'

Did this woman lack all inhibitions? 'Would you like to sit?'

They sat.

'I've been expecting to hear from you for days,' she said belligerently. 'I phoned the details of my new hotel but no one's been in touch.'

'Had there been anything of importance to tell you, I assure you we would immediately have informed you.'

'You're not going to learn anything until you take her disappearance seriously.'

'Mrs Ross, I have as many lads as possible trying to find out where she is. Every one of her known friends has been contacted, a dozen people have been interviewed, all possible leads have been followed.'

'Someone must know something.'

'Have you read the local newspaper?'

'No.'

'The news of Mrs Harvey's disappearance has been mentioned in it. I haven't seen the article, which is accompanied by a photograph of her, so I cannot say how factual it is, but at this stage that does not really matter, it is the publicity which counts. There is the chance one or more of the main newspapers will pick up the story and the fact of her disappearance will become nationally known. If Mrs Harvey has suffered an accident or an illness which caused her to lose her memory, it will become very much more likely she will be recognized.'

'You're saying you think that's what has happened?'

'It would explain why she failed to meet you or provide the information which would enable you to get in touch with her.'

'My question was, do you think that's what's happened?'

'Unfortunately, there isn't the evidence to form a strong judgment.'

'You're giving me the runaround. You think she's dead, murdered by her husband.'

'I assure you . . .'

'I've been to the farm. The housekeeper told me the concreting has been stopped on your orders. You think me a gullible colonial who can't work out what that means?'

'I had been hoping to avoid distressing you, Mrs Ross,

unless there was sufficient certainty to have to do so. I fear there is the possibility that Mrs Harvey is dead and her body is beneath the concrete.'

Her features worked as she struggled to keep her emotions under control. 'Murdered by him so he could keep those bloody cows.'

'Until we know, very sadly, that she is dead, we cannot determine whether or not she died from natural causes.'

'That's likely when she's been buried under the concrete?'

'However unlikely, we have to keep the possibility in mind. She might have suffered a fatal stroke in the presence of somebody and in circumstances that made him or her afraid that it would seem as if violence had been offered.'

'Why the hell isn't the concrete being ripped up to see if she is under it?'

'At the moment, we do not have the right to do that.'

She stood. 'There's none of you with the guts to do anything until someone says so.'

He watched her leave. No doubt in Australia, a detective inspector would have had the concrete ripped up before he questioned his authority to do so.

NINE

The pawnbroker round had been brief when there had been only the one pawnshop in Carnford. It had become longer when, due to the economic turmoil, a new one had been opened in the High Street. The two had similar work but a different trade. At Tetlers in the High Street, jewellery, gold, ceramics, coin and stamp collections and small antiques were pledged by those who had lost well paid jobs and could see little immediate chance of regaining employment; in the other pawnbroker, goods – often of small value – were brought in to tide over the householder until the next payday or, often, the next out-of-work allowance.

Miles walked down the High Street, stopped in front of the delicatessen. Did he take Irene to the cinema in Dawstone which had four screens, one of which was showing a film she wanted to see, or did he buy some Brie, her favourite cheese, for their supper? He decided on Brie. Her parents would be out that evening.

Small plastic shopping bag in one hand, he left the delicatessen and resumed walking past a saddler's – Irene dreamed of owning a horse – a gun shop – he wouldn't mind owning a pair of Royal Holland and Hollands – and a hairdresser before he reached Tetlers. The traditional three balls did not hang above the doorway; the interior could not be marked through the plate glass window because of thick net curtaining. The only indication as to what trade was carried on inside was provided by the printed notice which stated Tetlers were pleased to value items without charge. Discretion was important for the upper trade.

Inside was no bulletproof glass barrier between customer and the man behind the counter – that might exacerbate a feeling of embarrassment – but a metal safety screen could be dropped at the press of one of four buttons strategically sited.

Miles entered and the door automatically closed behind him.

''Morning, Constable. And a very good morning I hope you find it.' Kean, the manager, was a short and bouncy man, with a round, smiling face. He wore black coat, striped trousers and a tie equally out of current fashion since it was black with thin silver and green stripes. Only his eyes betrayed his true character; even when he smiled, they remained cold, suspicious and once described as the eyes of a spitting cobra.

Miles brought a printed sheet out of his pocket. 'The latest list of stolen valuables.' He handed it across the counter.

Kean quickly read the list. 'Nothing has come through here. It seems the fraternity have been less active than usual.'

'It's hard times even for the villains . . . Before I forget, there's one more robbery to add.' He had trouble finding a creased scrap of paper. 'Came through just as I was leaving. A pendant/brooch, Edwardian, platinum-topped fourteen carat gold, four large diamonds, eleven smaller ones, insured value five and a half thousand.'

'Just give me the details again while I write them down.'

Miles did as asked.

'Is there a photo of the pendant?'

'The owner never bothered to have one taken.'

'How was it stolen?'

'Came home from a drinks party, she took it off and left it on the dressing table while she went down to eat, returned to find it gone, the window open and a ladder against the wall.'

'People ask to become victims.'

'Or welcome a robbery because their baubles are over-insured.'

'Difficult to find a company who'll accept an unknown valuer's figures.'

'But not impossible.'

'A cynic?'

Miles smiled. 'It's better known in the force as experience.

By the way, is Bill around? I want to know if there will be a concert next month.'

'No doubt, pop, not classical. He's not here. I fear he has had to attend the funeral of his aunt.'

Miles smiled.

'A committed cynic! This time, without reason. Bill does have an aunt, she has just died, he has gone to her funeral because he's the nearest relative and was fond of her and she has – should I say had? – a set of six mahogany dining chairs which she always claimed were Hepplewhite.'

'Could they be?'

'Unlikely, but not impossible. I had a lady – to compliment her – who insisted very forcibly and vulgarly that her silver gilt dish was gold; yet when I was working at another branch, a man brought in a portrait miniature and wanted to know if it was good enough for a small loan. I was able to confirm the miniature was by Hilliard and therefore worth very much more than he believed and would enable him, if sold, to enjoy some of the fruits of life.'

'Some people have all the luck. I'll be on my way . . .'

'One moment. I should like you to know that a man came in here and it seemed to me he fitted the description of the husband in a photograph, which appeared in the local newspaper, of a couple, the wife of whom has disappeared. The photo was far from crystal clear, but there was a very distinct likeness. However, he gave me his name as Ackroyd.'

'What was he popping?'

'I prefer the expression valuing.'

'Sorry.'

'A nineteenth century gold cluster ring. Central diamond of no great value and eight small diamonds in the circle. There was an inscription. *Forever, together.*'

'What was it worth?'

'I valued it at four hundred pounds.'

'He took that?'

'After an unproductive attempt to make me raise the figure because it had cost eight hundred when he had bought it, he left with it.'

*   *   *

Miles entered Tyler's room in a rush. 'Sarge, I've just . . .'

'Barged in, like a herd of bloody elephants,' Tyler said sourly.

'I've been handing out the latest list of stolen jewellery and Kean, the manager at Tetlers, the pawnbroker in the High Street . . .'

'Tell me something more I know and succeed in wasting more of my time.'

'He's had a man, calling himself Ackroyd, who offered a ring.'

'Very unusual. Now if you've nothing better to do . . .'

'Kean reckons the man was Harvey.'

'Why?'

'Saw the photograph of him and his wife in the paper.'

'That wasn't clear enough for a solid identification.'

'He knows that, but still thinks it was Harvey. It must have been his wife's ring.'

Tyler stared into the past. One week after his wife had left him, the postman had brought a small package. It contained the ring he had bought her when they became engaged.

'Sarge, it's got to be hers.'

'There isn't any "must" in our job.'

'It's proof Harvey killed her.'

'It's proof of nothing more than that for one reason or another, Harvey – if it was he – had possession of his wife's ring – if it was his wife's.'

'You suppose she'd give it to him if she was alive?'

It could happen. 'Have you a description of the ring?'

'A diamond cluster with a central diamond and eight others round it. Harvey left with the ring because he wanted eight hundred and Kean wouldn't go beyond four.'

'Did he ask for identification?'

'Ackroyd gave his address before the bargaining began.'

'Have you checked it out?'

'There hasn't been time.'

'When was this?'

Silence.

'Didn't occur to you that timing could be important? Am

I being stupid to wonder if you asked what the ring was worth?'

'Kean offered four hundred which was six hundred short of what Harvey needed for the deposit which was why he wouldn't sell.'

'Anything more?'

'No.'

'Right.'

In other words, Miles thought resentfully as he left, clear off and do something useful.

He had misjudged Tyler, who went into the next room. Tait was talking over the phone and his expression when he saw Tyler was unwelcoming. 'What the hell is it this time?' He replaced the receiver.

'I've just had young Miles report, sir. He's been out on the pawnbrokers' round and Kean claims a man who called himself Ackroyd and tried to sell a ring was Harvey.'

Tait opened a drawer in his desk, brought out a packet of medicinal lozenges and put one in his mouth. 'Damned sore throat,' he said between sucks.

Tyler was not surprised by Tait's apparent lack of interest. An experienced officer liked to give the impression that no evidence was ever unexpected.

'Do we have a description of the ring?'

'A diamond cluster of no great value with an inscription.'

'When was this?'

'Miles didn't ask.'

'Not been instructed to do his job properly?'

Tyler silently swore.

Tait chewed and swallowed a second lozenge. 'They claim one of these will calm a sore throat for three to four hours. More likely three to four minutes . . . Why does Kean say the man was Harvey?'

'Recognized him from the photo in the local rag.'

'That was poor in detail, so we need a more definite identification. Get one.'

'Yes, sir. It's my guess the identification is good since Kean's a sharp old bird. If so, the deposit on the concreting was a thousand, so he'll do his damnedest to get more for the ring from another jeweller.'

'Check with his bank and find out what he's recently drawn.' Tait sat back in his chair. 'How do you see it?'

'I'm wondering how incriminating will it be if we can confirm the ring was his wife's?'

'You suggest a woman would willingly get rid of one of her rings?'

'It can happen,' Tyler said bitterly.

Tait looked briefly at him, was about to say something, checked the words.

TEN

As Dowling waited in the bank, seated on one of the four chairs for clients, he again recalled certain domestic incidents. When shopping in Tesco with Laura a month back, they had met a friend and her daughter. Laura had exclaimed over the curly golden hair, the deep blue eyes, the lovely smile. The previous week there had been a TV programme about older women having children and Laura had said, vehemently, that it was unfair to both child and mother. The previous evening they had been walking down Prade Street and she had stopped in front of a children's shop and commented on how pretty the dresses were inside. Baby noises? One of his mates had recently advised him that a newborn baby was like having the radio on full blast all night and that during the day one was waiting for the debt collector to turn up. Even so . . .

'Constable Dowling?' a woman said.

He came to his feet. She looked as if she regularly practised how to refuse a loan.

'These are the figures you want.'

He thanked her, took the sheet of paper. Six hundred pounds had been drawn from Harvey's account, leaving seventeen pounds forty-five.

Miles entered Tetlers. Kean stepped out of the office and stood behind the counter. 'Good morning, Constable Miles. More lists?'

'Not this time. It's about the ring Mr Ackroyd wanted to sell you. Or Mr Harvey, as you reckon he was.'

The welcoming smile remained, but the eyes expressed wariness.

'When was this?'

'It is of some importance?'

'It could be.'

'I hope there's no suggestion anything was out of order?'

'Not really, but the boss was wondering if you bothered to ask for identification beyond the address?'

Kean's smile dimmed. 'Since it was not a valuable ring, I judged the address to be sufficient.'

'You checked it was straight?'

'There are occasions, unfortunately becoming fewer and fewer, when one instinctively judges another to be honest. I so judged Mr Ackroyd. I only doubted my own judgment when I saw the photograph of Harvey in the local newspaper and the possibility of deception arose. In my defence, I can say without question that the ring was not on any of your lists and, regretfully, Homer sometimes sleeps. Perhaps it is a sign of old age . . .'

As Kean continued speaking, Miles decided Kean had had his doubts about the provenance of the ring, but business would have been business.

'So that's the way it was,' Kean concluded.

'Very understandable.'

'I am grateful for your understanding.'

Was that telling him he had sounded like a pretentious prick? Miles wondered. Still conscious of his youthful appearance, he had not yet fully accepted that being in the force added moral to the legal authority.

'I understand you wish to know when Mr Ackroyd, as I will continue to call him, brought this ring?

'If possible.'

'It would be a further mistake on my part if it were not.' He went into the office, soon returned. 'Monday, at eleven thirty-five o'clock. The address he gave was number thirty-eight, Hardtop Road.'

Jenner turned into Hardtop Road. There was no parking space outside No. 38, or for another seven houses. It was a rule of life that one could never park outside one's destination.

He stepped out of the car. This was an area of Carnford where the vagaries of wealth had, unusually, become marked by the varying houses; a modest semi-detached might be set next to a five bedroom detached house. He walked back past front gardens which had been turned into parking spaces and others which were full of colour. Carol was a keen gardener, he was not, but by the laws of the sexes, he spent time on hands and knees, weeding, planting, trimming, when he would have preferred to be in front of the television with a can of lager in his hand.

No. 38 was semi-detached, the front door with lead canopy stood between bay windows. Nineteen thirties, he guessed. The front door was opened by a woman whose face was heavily lined. He introduced himself, explained the reason for his visit.

'My name is Langford, not Ackroyd.'

'It may seem a silly question, but do you live here?'

She smiled. 'I do.'

He answered the unasked question. 'I wanted to have a word with Mr Ackroyd and was told he lived here.'

'I'm afraid not.'

'I wonder . . . Perhaps you could tell me if you know Mr and Mrs Thomas Harvey?'

She shook her head. 'I don't . . . but the name does seem familiar. Is he the poor man whose wife has disappeared?'

'That's right.'

'You're asking me questions because of her?'

'We're asking anyone and everyone in case they can help.'

'I wish I could, but I've never met them and I'm sure my husband hasn't either.'

'I didn't think you could have, seeing I'd been given the wrong address, but I had to make sure. I have a boss who wants every "i" dotted and every "t" crossed. Which means he's going to ask me how long you've lived here.'

'Only a few months.'

'Can you remember the name of the previous owner?'

'It's . . . Lost it! My memory sometimes seems to go walkabout. Are you ever sure you know something until you try to remember it?'

'Happens all the time.' He had a precise memory, but shared minor disabilities often encouraged a slight sense of comradeship.

'If the name's important, I could look through our papers and find it.'

'That would be very kind.'

'You think . . . I suppose I mustn't ask questions.'

He said lightly, 'You may ask, Mrs Langford, but I cannot answer.'

'Of course. Instead of standing there, come on in.'

The sitting room was comfortably furnished; on one wall were two framed paintings which immediately caught his attention.

'My husband's,' she said, noticing his interest. 'When he comes back from work, he likes to spend time painting because it clears his mind.'

And confuses the viewer's, he thought. Chaos unlimited. 'He's certainly talented.'

'He'd like to hear you say that! Do sit down while I go upstairs. I may be a little time because my husband does not believe in tidy files.'

He sat, staring at the paintings on either side of the blocked-up fireplace, wondered if her husband saw shape and form where others could not.

She returned. 'I found what I was looking for surprisingly quickly. The name's Smithson. I should have remembered the Smithsonian.'

'Have you any idea where they moved to?'

'It's probably not far away as they wanted to stay in this area. They had two children and a third was due, so they needed four bedrooms and there are only three here.'

'Do you have their address?'

'We didn't keep in touch.'

He sensed disapproval. 'How old is your telephone directory?'

'We had a new one a few weeks ago.'

'Their new address may be in there, then. May I look at it?'

The address was quickly found: Bellemaison, 15, Nerwent Crescent. He asked her where that was.

'Go down to the end of the road, turn left and it's the second . . . no, third on your right. In fact, it's not a crescent.

I've always wondered if the person who named it had elliptical eyesight.'

Moments later, he parked outside a large, detached house. On the gatepost was a carved name board which read Bellemaison. The front garden was patterned with small diamond shaped pockets of earth with dwarf flowers in them, surrounded by smoothed pebbles. He was not surprised that Sheila Smithson was thirty plus, trying to look twenty almost. Her two sons were overweight and undisciplined. The younger threw a small wooden brick at Jenner and was not corrected.

'What do you want?' she asked as she sat in one of the expensively upholstered and comfortable armchairs.

'Whether you know someone who . . .'

She interrupted him. 'We entertain a lot, so I expect we do. Last week, we had a barbecue for eighteen people. It was a great success.'

The elder boy pulled the younger one's hair. From upstairs came the sounds of crying.

'What is that silly girl doing with Catherine?' She stood, hurried upstairs.

The hair pulling ceased and the elder boy picked up another wooden brick and faced Jenner.

'Throw that at me and you'll get it back twice as hard,' Jenner said. His tone carried conviction.

Mrs Smithson returned to the sitting room before hostilities began. 'I've told her again and again, not to do that. I won't have her upsetting Catherine. Nursemaids really are impossible, aren't they?'

'Do you know Mr and Mrs Thomas Harvey?'

'James Harvey used to be a very good friend of ours. But then he married Susan. I don't like criticizing anyone, but she really is rather parvenu. We don't see them these days.'

He tried again. 'Mr and Mrs Thomas Harvey.'

'I wonder if they were the people we met just before we moved out of the other house. They had a name something like that. Dinkie introduced them to us. They really were the most extraordinary people. Reggie – he's my husband – works in the City at a very important job. Dinkie said they were farmers – I would never have thought so since she was dressed reasonably well and wore a charming diamond necklace; of course, they can't have been genuine diamonds, not with that sort of people. I can't think why Dinkie brought them. Reggie, who likes to know things, asked the man what was the expected return on capital in farming? That got him talking cows until I couldn't stand it any longer and started telling the woman about the wonderful barbecue parties I give. I buy only the finest quality meat – have it sent down from Scotland, of course. I can't think why, but I told them they must come to our next barbeque party and gave her one of my cards with the date of the next one written on it. She was very rude. Instead of telling me how much she'd like to come, said she'd be in touch if they were free that day . . . The more I think about it, the more certain I am their name was Harvey.'

'He was a dairyman?'

'I suppose one could call him that.'

'Did he say where he farmed?'

'Somewhere Without. I thought he was trying to be funny, but he said it really was the name.'

'Brecton Without.'

'That could be right. After all, only a farmer would live in somewhere called that.'

The boys had been quiet for long enough, so they began to fight. She asked them to stop and they ignored her. She spoke to Jenner and said they were very spirited, weren't they? He reckoned he was looking at two future clients of the police.

He returned to the car. Accept Mrs Smithson, then living in Hardtop Road, had been remembering correctly. She had been snubbed by the wife. Gillian Harvey would be a dab hand at snubbing. Surely the farmer who could talk only about cows had been Thomas Harvey. What other village was named Without? Here was the link between Harvey and Ackroyd. When asked for a name by the pawnbroker, he had given a prepared one. But when also asked for an address, he had been unprepared and, knowing he must not give his own address or that of one of his friends, he had remembered the obnoxious Smithson woman.

'Had a good holiday?'Tyler asked when Jenner entered the room.

'A couple of weeks in Jamaica, that's all, Sarge . . . Mrs Langford lives in Hardtop Road and knows nothing about the Harveys other than what she'd read in the papers or seen on the telly . . . Did you know the case had been mentioned on that?'

'Yes.'

'I didn't.'

'What you don't know would make the Encyclopedia Britannica seem pocket size . . . So the lead's a frost.'

'It would have been except for yours truly. Since the Langfords had only been in the house for a short while, I wondered if Harvey could have met or come across the previous owners and that's why he knew and used Hardtop Road as his fake address. I had a word with Mrs Smithson, who had been living there at the time. Tarty and stupid, with two young gangsters downstairs and a moll upstairs. She met a Harvey and wife at a party. She thought the wife was a bitch and the husband a complete bore because all he could talk about was cows. So when Harvey sold the ring and had to give an address that seemed safe, he recalled the Smithsons – no doubt with an inward shudder – and used the address on their card. Neat bit of work on my part, eh?'

ELEVEN

Tait, his mind elsewhere, let the pencil in his fingers drop down on to the desk. The lead point broke. 'This woman doesn't sound very positive the couple were the Harveys. Have you questioned the friend? What was her name?'

'Dinkie,' Tyler replied.

'I'm glad I don't know anyone by that name. Has she been asked if Thomas Harvey was at the party?'

'Not yet.'

'That seems to have become the stock answer when I ask if something has been done.'

There was a brief silence.

'Then until she is asked, it must remain an assumption that it was Harvey.'

'Surely the coincidence of a bitch of a wife and a husband who can only talk about cows is off the scale of probability?'

'You have not yet accepted that many coincidences turn out to be nothing of the sort, they are merely facts you have chosen to connect. We need confirmation. When we have that, I will probably ask the super to agree it's time to bring in SOCO.'

'To dig up the concrete?'

'To find the evidence that will warrant our doing that.'

Dowling turned the car's engine off and belched. He should not have persuaded the younger of the women who served in the canteen to give him a second serving of fried onion. He left the car, crossed the pavement, walked up to the front door. Bellemaison. With a name like that, it hadn't been necessary for Frank to warn him about the Smithson woman. He rang the bell.

She opened the door. 'Yes?'

He identified himself.

'Must you people keep bothering me?'

Officers were required to treat all members of the public with respect. Dowling respected only those he had reason to; a woman of assumed superiority was not one of them. 'It's not by choice.'

Her lips tightened. 'Why are you here?'

'To ask you who Dinkie is.'

'That's none of your business.'

'On the contrary. I need to know her identity.'

'I have no intention of telling you.'

'You would prefer to come to the police station to tell me?'

'You . . . you're threatening to arrest me?' she asked shrilly, aghast at the thought of suffering the embarrassment of the sneering amusement of friends when they learned what had happened.

'Offering to save you trouble if you give me her name.'

'I . . . Dorinda Drury.'

'Where does she live?'

After a moment, she said, 'Fairfax Road.'

'What is the name or number of the house?'

'Fourteen.'

He returned to his car. A clod of earth, thrown by one of the sons, hit the door.

No. 14 was smaller than the house he had just left, but of the same period. With the pet name of Dinkie, he had expected Mrs Drury to be a second Mrs Smithson, but she had reached middle age without any attempt to hide the fact. She asked him into the sitting room and offered him coffee, which he politely refused.

'You're suggesting I might be able to help you find Mrs Harvey?' she asked, once he had explained the reason for his visit.

'I'm hoping so.'

'I can't think how, but of course, I'll do whatever I can. You're asking about the Mr and Mrs Harvey we met at a party the Smithsons gave just before they moved. I can't think why Mary thought *we* brought them to the party. My husband and I had just been talking to them until it was considered time we should meet someone else and were moved on. We'd found them interesting and I suggested to Mary that she meet them. Unfortunately, she thought him boring and his wife, rude.'

'Did you learn what his Christian name was?'

'Thomas, the same as my brother's.'

'And her Christian name?'

'I think it was Gillian, but I can't be certain.'

'He spoke about his work?'

She laughed. 'He kept cows, loved cows, and probably dreamed cows. He was so enthusiastic that he invited us to see his herd of peerless animals some time. We meant to take up the invitation, but haven't managed to do so yet.'

'Presumably he gave you the name of his farm and where-abouts it was?'

'I don't remember the name of the farm, but I do the village. Brecton Without.'

He thanked her.

'I haven't been able to help you at all, have I?'

'On the contrary, you may have done,' he answered.

'There doesn't seem to be much doubt,' Kirby said over the phone.

If there had been, he would have been criticized, Tait thought resentfully.

'And are you saying that this link between the false address given to the pawnbroker and Harvey provides the proof necessary to warrant the excavation of the concrete base?'

'Unfortunately, I don't think it does.'

'Then what do you propose?'

'That SOCO searches the house and grounds. They may find sufficient probability of murder to provide the proof we now lack.'

'Has there been no search?'

'By us, of course, sir, but that was when the evidence of murder was very far from compelling.'

'You are admitting the search was incompetently carried out?'

'Far from it. But my lads are not trained to the degree that scene of crime officers are and with all the out-buildings offering dozens of hiding places for a body, they did their best; it's just that SOCO may be able to do better.'

'A poor excuse.'

Tait replaced the receiver, scratched his ear and winced at the sharp bolt of pain. His doctor could not explain why this should suddenly occur and the previous year had suggested it was a temporary nerve reaction that would cease. It hadn't. His doctor had then suggested he cease scratching his ear.

He stared through the window at ancient oak trees in a garden on the other side of the road, then used the internal phone to tell Tyler to organize SOCO's search. 'And that means every square inch.'

'That's a tall order, Guv, when you remember the huge bales of hay and all the straw.'

'He may have cut her up and reckoned a bale would be a great place for all the bits and pieces.'

'But bad for the hay or straw.'

'You are a comic?'

'No, sir.'

'Then don't attempt to become one. The bales can be left until we are certain there is nowhere else which might produce evidence.'

The six man SOCO team, wearing white paper overalls, mouth masks, gloves and search shoes, began their work in the attic of the farmhouse. The overflow central heating and domestic water tanks were checked by torchlight, the laborious task of searching the pellet insulation was carried out. It was late afternoon before the team moved down to the top floor. There were four bedrooms and one bath-room. In the bathroom, handbasin and bath emptying and overflow gratings and plugs were examined for any indi-cation of blood stains, then the two cane Ali Baba baskets were emptied of dirty clothes. There was a stained towel in the second basket. Filter papers were rubbed on the stains; the substance which had been transferred on to the papers was treated with drops from three reagents. Blood.

The towel was folded and placed in an exhibit bag, sealed and the sergeant noted on the label the date, time and location, and the name of the officer who found it. No other item of clothing was stained. A focussed search for material which could offer DNA comparison was made; a comb in one of the cupboards had several black hairs, three of which had roots.

The sergeant ordered a PC to find someone who could say what colour hair the missing woman had. The PC returned to report Mrs Spens said it was black. The comb was dropped into an exhibit bag and the identifying label written.

A PC drove to the nearest Home Office forensic laboratory with the exhibits.

Kirby left the car and crossed to the farmhouse. Tait met him at the front door. 'The towel and hairs are with the lab?' Kirby asked, as if he considered it quite possible they had not yet been sent.

Tait looked at his watch. 'They'll have been there for a time, if the roads haven't been choc-a-block.'

'You've said it's priority?'

'Yes.' Tait had not bothered to do so. At the laboratory, all work was priority and nothing would have been gained by naming their exhibits as such. 'The towel was on top of a half-full basket of women's underclothes. Assuming Mrs Harvey typically changed her underwear every day, it would seem the towel was placed there on the day she disappeared. That does raise the question, why didn't Harvey put it straight into the washing machine?'

'Did the housekeeper deal with dirty clothes?'

'Mrs Spens says Mrs Harvey always put her clothes into the basket, but left Mrs Spens to take them out and have them washed. SOCO have checked the walls and floor of bathroom and bedroom and found no traces. Perhaps he strangled her and blood, but no other traces, were expelled in the course of her death. It's unusual, but it can happen. I remember a woman who bit through her tongue as she was strangled and there was blood, but nothing more. Death doesn't always follow the textbook.'

'Have you questioned Harvey again?'

'I've been waiting . . .'

'For Godot?'

'For you to be here, sir.'

'We'll speak to him now,' Kirby said sharply.

'I'll get one of the lads to find him.'

Harvey, hair and clothing littered with chaff and dust, arrived.

'How much longer am I going to have to suffer this constant interference?' he demanded.

'As you must realize . . .' Kirby began.

'Do you give a damn about what you're doing with your absurd accusation that I killed my wife? Mrs Spens says she's leaving because she couldn't work here any more. I went up to the village shop and one of the old biddies said I shouldn't be allowed in there. June, in the post office, always used to have a chat, now doesn't say a word unless she has to; when I give her money for letters or a parcel, she handles it as if it may be carrying the plague. You've turned me into a pariah.'

'We are only doing our duty.'

'The country's become a police state where you hound innocent people?'

'When necessary, we determine whether there is innocence or guilt.'

'My wife leaves me because she has discovered I'm having an affair. You can't trace her, so I have to be guilty of having murdered her.'

'You have not been accused of murder.'

'And that inference has not been made? Not when you people tried to browbeat Mrs Gillmore into saying I was so desperate to marry her, I would do anything to get rid of my wife?'

'Mrs Gillmore was treated with respect and no attempt was made to browbeat her.'

'If you're not accusing me of anything, why have you searched my house?'

'Mr Harvey, am I correct in saying you have paid the deposit of a thousand pounds so that the concrete could be laid?'

'Yes.'

'How did you pay? Was it by cheque or by cash?'

'Cash.'

'How were you in possession of so much?'

'Perhaps I printed it.'

'You have very recently withdrawn six hundred pounds from your bank, which virtually emptied your account.'

'You've been even more outrageously intrusive than I thought.'

'Where did the other four hundred come from?'

'My friend lent it to me.'

'The same friend who was going to finance the whole barn?'

'Yes.'

'Will you give me his name so that we can ask him to confirm what you have just said?'

'No.'

'Why not?'

'I've answered that question a dozen times. I'm not having him dragged into this mess.'

'When all he is asked to do will be to confirm your evidence, he will have been dragged nowhere.'

'You will be tact personified? No more than half a dozen armed policemen in order to avoid arousing the perverse interest of neighbours?'

'Have you recently visited Tetlers, the pawnbrokers in High Street?'

Harvey failed to conceal the uneasy surprise the question caused. 'When they won't accept a cow as a pledge?'

'You have not taken a ring there to sell?'

'No.'

'Giving the name of Ackroyd?'

'No.'

'Mr Kean, the manager of Tetlers, has identified you as the man who named himself Ackroyd.'

'He should drink less.'

'You gave him your address as thirty-eight, Hardtop Road. Have you ever visited a house in Hardtop Road?'

'Never heard of it until now.'

'Mr and Mrs Drury met you and your wife there at a party given by Mr and Mrs Smithson. They were impressed by your dedication to dairy farming.'

'This is all crap.'

'I doubt you have ever previously been in a pawnbrokers, so were unprepared to be asked to give an address. To give a false one on the spur of the moment is a surprisingly difficult thing to do. In the panic, knowing hesitation would cause suspicion, you remembered that party and the address of where it was given.'

'You're weaving webs out of moonshine.'

'How would the pawnbroker have been given the address except from you?'

'From someone who had previously pawned something.'

'Mr Kean's books show there has been no such person,' Kirby said, gaining brief, muted respect from Tait because of the authority with which he lied. 'What did you try to sell?'

'How many times do I have to tell you . . .'

'I will answer my own question. It was a diamond cluster ring. There was a centre diamond of not very great value and eight smaller diamonds surrounding this. Do you remember it?'

'Why the hell should I?'

'You would not like to revise your answer?'

'No.'

'Have you tried to sell it to any other jeweller?'

'Not to any jeweller because there is no such ring.'

Kirby stood. 'Every prevarication, every lie, must count against you.'

'And as I am learning, truth is the most damning of all.'

They left. In the car, Kirby started the engine, said, 'Not breaking easily.'

'Would one expect a man of his character to do so?'

Kirby, annoyed by the inference in that remark, let the clutch out too sharply and stalled the engine.

TWELVE

Dawstone, the county capital, was divided by the river Daw, along the banks of which were some of the oldest properties in the city. Once noted for its flourishing market, it was now remarked only for its shopping centre, traffic jams and sadistic traffic wardens.

DC Plumpton – he had to suffer considerable ribbing because of his name and his waist size – walked into Georges & Son, jewellers in Molehill Street. The young woman behind one counter smiled a welcome, the middle aged man, Adams, behind the other counter nodded.

'Suppose I raise my offer to a hundred?' Plumpton asked cheerfully.

Adams wearily shook his head. Whenever Plumpton entered the shop, he offered to buy – for a tenth of its cost – the engagement ring in the centre of the display in the window. For Adams, there had never been any humour in the absurd offer.

'Oh, well, I'll have to take my custom elsewhere.'

That I should be so lucky, Adams thought. 'I can help you in some way?'

'We're asking all the jewellers in the area if they can recognize a piece of jewellery. It may have been bought some years ago or very recently have been offered for sale.'

'Where's the photo?'

'There isn't one.'

'Helpful!'

'It's described as an eighteenth century diamond cluster ring. The central diamond is not very large or of good quality and the surrounding eight diamonds are much smaller.'

'How many carats is the main one?'

'I've no idea.'

'The cut?'

'Of what?'

'The central diamond.'

'I haven't been told that either.'

'I am tempted to mention needles and haystacks.'

'There is one more thing. It was engraved with Forever Together, or some such mush.'

'You are obviously of the modern generation for whom romance is not cool, but cold.'

'Could you have sold it? It's odds on it was bought somewhere in the area.'

'When?'

'Maybe a little over nine years ago.'

'A cluster ring of no great quality, engraved with old fashioned sentimentality . . . I have the shadow of a memory, but nothing more. We have not been offered such a ring.'

'It's a bit steep expecting anyone to remember, but it would help us a load . . .'

'The only real possibility of our being in a position to identify it is if we were asked to have the engraving carried out. Then the fact will be somewhere in the books if my assistant managed to remember the procedure.'

'I wasn't here those years ago,' the young lady said.

'Your predecessor was very like you, Miss Easten.'

'That's not fair.'

'If your shadowy memory is valid, let's hope the ring was bought here and there's the record of the engraving being done,' Plumpton said, breaking into the budding argument. He handed across a card. 'Give me a buzz on the phone if you strike gold . . . In the circumstances that's rather sharp, isn't it!'

Adams offered no comment. Miss Easten winked at Plumpton as he left.

Tyler entered Tait's room. 'We've heard from Dawstone. One of the jewellers there has not been offered the ring, but has a very vague memory of a ring that could fit the description.'

'Doesn't sound promising.'

'It depends on whether they carried out the engraving.'

'With the way things are going, they won't have done.' Tait went to rub his ear, remembered not to do so and dropped his hand. 'For the first time in a while, I had to buy a few things at the supermarket last night. They cost a fortune.'

'Everything does these days.'

'And in another few years, if we don't have some luck, people will talk about how cheap things were now . . . How long before we hear from Dawstone again?'

'They promised to get back on to us the moment they have anything to say.'

'Grab a chair.'

'I . . . Sorry, sir?'

'Sit down, man, and tell me your thoughts on the case.'

Tyler, surprised, sat. Normally, Tait was uninterested in the opinions of others. Kirby must be riding him very roughly.

The phone rang. Harvey slumped in an easy chair, awoke. The caller would be one more damned reporter wanting to ask loaded questions, the answers to which would be twisted to brand him a murderer in a way that left him unable to claim libel. The ringing ceased.

He stared across the room at the mantelpiece on which now stood the early eighteenth century Yorkshire pearlware cow with milkmaid which he had bought after winning his first award at a show. Second in the heifer class. Gillian had refused to have it in the sitting room or dining room because she had more than enough of cows without having one stare at her all day. It had remained in a drawer until she had demanded separate bedrooms, then he had had it on the dressing table in his. Now, because of her absence, it was back where it had started. But where was he?

The phone rang again. He stood, crossed to the open doorway, went into the hall and across to the corner cupboard on which the phone stood. 'Yes?' he said aggressively, waiting for the first loaded question.

'Tom, what's the matter? What's happening?' Helen's voice expressed her worry. 'I've phoned and phoned and there's been no answer.'

'I've been coping with a threatened outbreak of mastitis so I've been in the sheds most of the time.'

'Why hasn't Mrs Spens answered?'

'She's gone.'

'Where?'

'Wherever housekeepers go when they are no longer willing to endure the infamy of living with a murderer.'

'Stop talking like that. Did she leave today?'

'No.'

'Then what did you have for lunch?'

'A tin of something – corned beef or spam, I suppose.'

'You can't remember which and probably had nothing else with it. I'm coming over to cook you a proper meal.'

'Keep away as far as possible from here or you'll be caught up in the mess.'

'Haven't I been caught up?'

'Then, you were just over-friendly with a farmer.'

'I wasn't, I was in love with him and am even more so now.'

'Can't you understand?'

'No.'

'The more obvious it becomes that we want to be together, the more certain the police will be that I arranged we should.'

'You didn't harm her, you couldn't, so no one can ever prove you did.'

'Innocence and proof aren't always bedfellows.'

'What food is there in the house?'

'I'm not certain.'

'Then I'll bring something with me.'

'Please don't . . .' The connection was cut.

Tyler noted the date on the tabloid he had bought on the way to divisional HQ. The previous evening, he had accepted it was one day short of the evening he had returned home to find the brief, cruel note which his wife had written before she left home. When he had woken up this morning, he had forgotten the anniversary. Seeing the date in black print reminded him. How long before that memory no longer had the power to spear his mind? Friends suggested he find himself another woman. So that he could be betrayed a second time? The phone interrupted his unhappy thoughts.

'Stitchworth lab here.'

'Sergeant Tyler.'

'Test results show the stain on the towel recovered from Tanton Farm was human blood.'

'Is there a match of DNA?'

'It'll be a time yet before that comes through.'

'Then you can't say anything more?'

'Only when I'm given the time to do so. The blood type is O, the most common.'

'It would be.'

'Life was never meant to be easy.'

A few words later, Tyler replaced the receiver. Did he report to the DI before he had learned what Harvey's blood group was? Probably save moans if he didn't.

He went into the CID general room, signed his name in the movement book and the reason for his leaving the station, and made his way down to the cars to find the CID Fiesta was out. He crossed to his own Clio, opened the driving door, stepped in, sat, picked out the small notebook in the glove locker and noted down the present mileage, as required in any claim for expenses.

He drove out of Carnford and the black clouds in his mind began to lift when he reached the countryside. God made the countryside, man made the town. He passed through Brecton Without and reached Tanton Farm. Surrounded by farmland, woodland, space, hearing the sounds of animals; not the ugly growl of traffic. As near to Nirvana as man should wish himself.

He left the car, crossed to the front door of the farm-house, knocked. The door opened and he faced Helen Gillmore. It hadn't, he thought, taken her long to move in. ''Morning, Mrs Gillmore, sorry to bother you. Is Mr Harvey around?'

'As far as I know, he's in the cowshed.'

'I'll find him.'

He walked across to the farm buildings, wondering how

she accepted that Harvey had killed in order for them to be together. Or did she enjoy the fortune of being able to shut her mind to what she did not wish to accept? In the dairy, Wade had washed down the concrete floor and was now sweeping the water away with a squeegee. He came to a stop by a corner of the large stainless steel tank in which the milk was cooled before it was collected by the milk lorry.

'I'm looking for Mr Harvey,' Tyler said.

'He ain't here,' was the sullen answer.

'So where is he?'

'With the young stock.'

'Where do they live?'

'In the field.'

'Which one?'

Wade indicated to the right.

Button-lipped even for a countryman, and uneasy, Tyler thought as he left the dairy and began to walk around the buildings. Worried by the presence of the police because he helped himself to milk? Wouldn't he be granted a daily ration of two, three pints? More likely, he was showing the common, stupid resentment of authority.

Harvey was in the centre of a five acre field down to grass in which a herd of animals was grazing. His expression was bitter as Tyler approached. Hoping to lighten the meeting, Tyler said, 'Nice looking cows.'

'Heifers.'

Farmers could be as taciturn as their labourers. 'Can you say what your blood group is?'

'Why?'

'Is there a reason why you should not want us to know?'

'No.'

'Then what group is it?'

Harvey moved away and visually inspected a heifer as it grazed the thick lay. He returned. 'A.'

'Thanks.'

'For what? Making public a bit more of myself?'

An odd way of putting it. Tyler said goodbye, returned to his car by the farmhouse, and drove off.

Back in the station, he was about to go into his room when Tait hurried along the corridor.

'Where the hell have you been? Your room was empty and no one knew where you were.'

'I made an entry in my movement book, sir. You can't have had the chance to read it.' Having spoken more ironically than intended, he hurriedly added, 'I had Stitchworth on the blower earlier . . .'

Tait passed Tyler, went in to his room and sat behind the desk. 'Am I allowed to hear what they had to say or do I have to await your pleasure?'

Never succumb to the pleasure of tweaking the dragon's tail, Tyler thought as he came to a stop. 'The blood on the towel was human and type O.'

'Has anyone thought to find out what Harvey's group is?'

'A.'

'Has the lab carried out a DNA test to determine whether the blood was the wife's?'

'They haven't had time to complete the work.'

'So there's no certainty it is hers.'

'Who else but Harvey is going to go into the bathroom and drop a bloodied towel into the basket she used since we know Mrs Spens didn't? Do we need a signed confession?'

'That's all.'

Tyler returned to his room, sat. Tait could never be described as friendly, but the pressure of the present case . . . He had forgotten to pass on the news about Mrs Gillmore. He reluctantly returned to the DI's room.

'What the devil is it?'

'When I went to Tanton Farm, sir, to find out what Harvey's blood group was, he wasn't at the farmhouse . . .'

'You intend to tell me where else he wasn't?'

'But Mrs Gillmore was there.'

'Thoughtful of you to bother to tell me.'

Tyler turned to leave.

'Was she just visiting for a bit of nookie or has she moved in?'

'I couldn't be certain, but gained the impression she was there to stay.'

'Not worried by a murder? Love really is blind when eyes are tight shut.'

Miles was about to return home and then spend the evening with Irene and her parents when the phone on Dowling's desk rang. Since Jenner sat at the next desk, Miles presumed he would answer the call and walked towards the door.

'Are you deaf?' Jenner asked.

'I thought you'd cope.'

'Erk's jobs are done by the erk.'

It was quicker and easier to answer the call than argue that juniority was not servitude. He crossed to the desk and lifted the receiver.

'Carter here, C division. Re: the ring you asked us to trace. Adams, the jeweller, has been able to confirm he both sold and engraved the ring in question. His records show he was asked to inscribe the ring with the words Forever Together and the bill was paid by cheque. The name was TG Harvey. How does that fit?'

'Like an over-tight necktie,' Miles answered.

A copy of Harvey's photograph was faxed to C division together with the request that it be shown to Adams to confirm, if possible, that this was the TG Harvey who had bought the ring and had it inscribed. Confirmation was given. Within an hour, there was a call from A Division. A diamond cluster ring, engraved Forever Together, had recently been bought by Clintons, in Stonebridge, for four hundred pounds.

THIRTEEN

Tait spoke to Kirby over the phone. 'The evidence proves Harvey bought the ring some years before, recently tried to sell it in this town, wasn't offered what he hoped, tried to sell it in Stonebridge and eventually had to accept the same amount he had previously refused.'

'But not that he had given that ring to his wife.'

'The presumption has to be strong. He bought it not far short of nine years ago, which would have been when he became engaged.'

'When did he first meet his wife and Mrs Gillmore?'

Tait did not answer.

'You could take the trouble to find out.'

'Yes, sir.'

The call over, Tait went into Tyler's office. 'I want to know when Mrs Harvey and Mrs Gillmore first met Harvey.'

'Just at the moment, sir, that's a bit difficult because . . .'

'You think an order is negotiable?' He returned to his own room, his previous resentment at Kirby's manner slightly eased by his ability to annoy a junior.

Tyler looked into the CID general room and found it empty, went down to the canteen and across to where Miles sat at a table with two PCs. 'There's no one upstairs.'

'That's because . . .'

'You consider your stomach more important than your job? Find out when Mrs Gillmore first met Harvey and also when his wife did.'

'Right Sarge; as soon as I've finished, I'll . . .'

'Do it now.' Tyler's resentment at Tait's manner became eased.

Miles scooped up a forkful of shepherd's pie, ate this as he left the canteen and went up the stairs to ground level, out of the building and across to the CID Fiesta. He drove out of Carnford and along lanes to Tanton Farm.

When he stepped out of the car on to the gravel, his mood lifted. Only a few puffballs of cloud floated in the sky, the sunshine was hot, the wind was but a zephyr, and he and Irene were going to a disco in the evening.

Harvey opened the front door.

'DC Miles, county . . .'

'Well?'

'I'd like a word if it's convenient.'

'It isn't. I'm eating lunch.'

'Then you're lucky,' Miles said, without having meant to speak.

'Really?'

'It's just . . . I had to come here before I'd finished my meal.'

'It seems we all suffer from unwelcome interruptions.'

'There are only one or two questions I have to ask . . .'

'Then ask them.'

'When did you first meet your wife?'

'A time ago.'

'Could you give a date?'

'The answer is important only to her and me.'

'I'm afraid we need to know.'

'The investigation into a crime which has not been committed demands the answer to one more impertinent and extraneous question?'

'Sorry, Mr Harvey, but I have been told to ask.'

'Nine years ago.'

'When did you first meet Mrs Gillmore?'

'Are you about to date all my friendships and acquaintances? . . . Two to three years ago.'

'You can't be more specific?'

'No.'

'Perhaps Mrs Gillmore could be.'

'Why should she?'

'Women are better at remembering that sort of thing.'

'And if she is?'

'May I ask her?'

'For God's sake . . . I suppose you'd better come in and ask or we'll have you standing there until you interrupt our tea.'

Miles followed Harvey into the dining room.

'Your meal's almost cold . . .' Helen began, stopped as she saw Miles. 'Hullo. It's Constable Miles, isn't it?'

'That's right, Mrs Gillmore.'

'So what brings you here?'

Harvey answered her. 'His lunch was interrupted so he decided it would be amusing to come and interrupt ours.'

Miles said hurriedly, 'I'm afraid I had no choice about the time I came here, Mrs Gillmore. My sergeant ordered me to drive over immediately.'

'A fire-breathing dragon?'

'A few sparks now and then.'

She smiled.

'If it won't inconvenience you too greatly,' Harvey said, 'would you care to ask your question and then leave us to finish our meal before it congeals?'

'Don't fuss, Tom,' she said. 'I have finished and while I'm being asked whatever it is, you can eat.' She turned to Miles. 'What is the question?'

'When did you first meet Mr Harvey?'

'Things become curiouser and curiouser. It was on the fourteenth of July, three years ago, at an agricultural show when Tom had just won an award.'

'Thank you and I apologize for interrupting your meal.'

Harvey spoke to Miles. 'You know the way out.'

Miles left. The roast pork and crackling, roast potatoes, and runner beans had looked and smelled delicious.

'I should have waited a while before going to see the Harveys,' Miles said in Tyler's room.

'Why?'

'I interrupted their meal and that got right up Mr Harvey's nose. But Mrs Gillmore was charming. I'm sure she doesn't . . .' He stopped.

'What?'

'I suppose I'll sound real soft when I say she has such a warm character, she couldn't . . . She can't believe he killed his wife or she'd have nothing to do with him.'

Tyler spoke quietly. 'I understand what you're saying and

when I had your experience, I'd likely have thought the same. But instinctive judgment of a person's nature has a poor record. I knew a man who was friendly, full of jokes, the first to shout a round of beer, married to a charming woman. She was rushed to hospital with two broken ribs and a bruised liver because he had a habit of bashing her and that time had gone too far. And what made even less sense was her in court, pleading for him. The bastard got two years – I'd have given him ten. So now you can tell me what you learned.'

'They met three years ago, on the fourteenth of July.'

'So the ring was bought for the wife and not for her!'

Tait and Jenner entered the middle interview room in divisional HQ. On one side of the table sat Harvey and Pascell, a robust man with a round and jolly face which belied his character, dressed in traditional black jacket, striped trousers, stiff collar and sober tie. There had been solicitor Pascells in Carnford for the past eighty-five years.

Tait said good morning, switched on the tape recorder and detailed time, place and who was present.

'My client,' Pascell said, his speech slow and precise, 'feels that having to come here is further police harassment.'

'He has been questioned no more often than has been necessary in the effort to try to locate his wife,' Tait replied. 'Asking him to come here is normal practice.'

'The questioning has been constant despite the fact that, from the beginning, my client has made it clear he knows only that his wife has disappeared.'

'We have to examine all the circumstances surrounding Mrs Harvey's disappearance.'

'Repeatedly asking the same questions cannot be termed necessary.'

'It can when we are not satisfied with the answers we receive.'

'It is my client's contention that as he has always told the truth, it is a gross misjudgment to refuse to believe him.'

'Mr Harvey has been asked here today to enable us to determine what the truth is.'

Pascell took the accusation of harassment no further.

'Mr Harvey, have you ever bought a ring from a jewellers in Dawstone called Georges and Son?'

'I bought my engagement ring in Dawstone, but I can't remember where.'

'Did you have it engraved before you presented it to your fiancée?'

'Yes.'

'What was the engraving?'

'I . . . I think it was something like eternity.'

'Forever together?'

'Probably.'

'My client has not accepted the ring under discussion is the engagement ring he bought,' Pascell said.

'Since he paid by cheque, the details of which are in the records of the jeweller's, it seems it must have been.'

'You have a copy of the records?'

'Not here.'

'Ah!' Pascell said, as if he had gained an important point.

'To return to the question, Mr Harvey,' Tait said. 'Have you at any time tried to pawn this ring at Tetlers, the pawn-broker in the High Street of this town?'

'No.'

'Perhaps you would like to reconsider your answer?'

'My client has no need to do so,' Pascell said.

'I would suggest to the contrary.'

'There is no necessity for him to respond to a policeman's suggestion.'

'Mr Harvey, following the disappearance of your wife, Mr Kean, manager at Tetlers, reported you had come in to his shop and tried to sell a ring. Is that correct?'

Harvey did not answer.

'Mr Kean was shown a photograph of you and he iden-tified you as the person who had wished to sell a diamond cluster ring. He described it as of no great value, added it had been engraved on the inside with "Forever Together". Both ring and engraving were paid for by cheque and the cheque was in your name. That was your wife's engage-ment ring, wasn't it?'

Pascell spoke to Harvey in a whisper.

'Yes,' Harvey answered.

'It was your wife's ring and you tried to sell it at Tetlers, but decided you were not being offered enough?'

'Yes.'

'It is unfortunate that you have seen fit to deny the fact until forced to admit it . . . Mr Harvey, why have you lied when asked if you attempted to sell the ring?'

'Isn't it obvious?' Harvey said harshly.

'I am afraid not.'

'I was too bloody ashamed to admit what happened.'

'Your sense of shame has been greater than the risk of being shown to be a liar?'

'Yes.'

'Do you still have the ring?'

'No.'

'Where is it now?'

'I took it to another pawnbroker to find out if I could get more.'

'You belatedly realized the danger of repeating your exposure to the ring locally?'

'My client made it quite clear what was his motive,' Pascell said.

'Very well. Mr Harvey, you were offered four hundred pounds in Tetlers. What were you offered in another jeweller's?'

'Four hundred.'

'You gained nothing by the second attempt?'

'No.'

'Presumably, you needed money to pay the deposit on the cost of the work on the foundations of a feed barn at your farm?'

'Yes.'

'But you were still six hundred pounds short. Where did that come from?'

'My bank.'

'Have you considered the consequences of being found to have had possession of your missing wife's engagement ring?'

'Are you trying to suggest . . .'

'Leave them to make the suggestions,' Pascell hurriedly said.

'Did your wife return her ring to you?' Tait asked.

'Not in the way you mean.'

'What do I mean?'

'My client,' Pascell said, 'cannot be conversant with your thoughts.'

'Then he is fortunate. Mr Harvey, how did you come by it if she did not hand it to you?'

'She threw it at me.'

'Overarm or underhand?'

'Are you mocking my client?' Pascell demanded.

'Expressing difficulty in believing what he tells me,' Tait replied. 'Mr Harvey, I will ask you again, how did you gain possession of your wife's ring?'

'I will reply again, she threw it at me.'

'Why?'

Pascell spoke to Harvey in a murmur.

'We had been rowing,' Harvey said.

'Over what?'

'She'd learned about my friendship with Mrs Gillmore. She took the ring off her finger, told me it was sufficiently cheap and nasty for my girlfriend, and threw it at me.'

'That must have been humiliating.'

'Inspector, kindly allow my client, not you, to give his evidence,' Pascell said.

'Mr Harvey, how did you react to what your wife had done?'

'I picked the ring up.'

'What were your emotions?'

'I can't remember.'

'You must have been very annoyed.'

'Probably more surprised.'

'Was she wearing other rings?'

'Yes.'

'Did she throw them at you as well?'

'No.'

'What were the other rings?'

'Her wedding ring and the diamond solitaire she bought herself after coming into her inheritance and one of her friends made a sneering remark about her tiny engagement ring.'

'Where is that solitaire ring now?'

'On her finger.'

'You are certain?'

'She never removed it.'

'Is it valuable?'

'I imagine it must be.'

'You have not tried to sell or pawn it?'

'My client,' Pascell said, 'has made it clear he has no knowledge of the ring's whereabouts beyond when he last saw it on her finger.'

'Unfortunately, we have learned your client's words have to be doubted.'

'You have evidence this solitaire diamond ring is not on a finger of Mrs Harvey?'

'No.'

'You have evidence my client has tried to sell or to pawn it, or has otherwise had possession of it?'

'No.'

'Then you have no reason to imply that he has.'

'Mr Harvey,' Tait said, 'what were your feelings when your wife bought and wore an expensive ring because the engagement ring you had given her was of small significance to her?'

'I don't remember. My feelings now are regret that I paid more for it than I could afford at the time.'

'You were not angry and insulted?'

'Inspector,' Pascell said in silky tones, 'do you wish to add outraged, infuriated and embittered?'

Tait spoke to Harvey. 'Have you recently told Mr Bushell you would like him to do more than merely construct the foundation/floor – that you would like him to erect the feed barn as well?'

'No.'

'He will confirm that you have not?'

'My client cannot answer for Mr Bushell,' Pascell said.

'He can say whether he believes there will be confirmation.'

'He cannot be asked to suppose another's response. Have you any more questions – relevant questions?'

'I think not for the present.'

'Then we will leave.'

Tait spoke into the tape recorder, ending the interview and giving the time. Jenner switched it off, extracted the two tapes and handed these to Tait, who signed them, and handed one to Pascell.

When they were on their own, Jenner said, 'Lawyers give me the guts ache.'

'If that's all, you're bloody lucky,' was Tait's reply.

FOURTEEN

The day was overcast, rain was forecast, and the wind had a touch of autumn. In the washroom at the end of the CID floor, Tait looked in the mirror over a handbasin and tried to convince himself he was not becoming balder. Normally sceptical, he had been lured into buying a treatment which would grow hair on a head as smooth as a boiled egg (as was portrayed on the TV). He would have liked to have charged the advertisers under the trade description acts.

Tyler looked in, saw Tait, and stepped inside. 'We've just heard from the lab, Sir. They've managed to gain a match. The blood on Mrs Harvey's towel was hers. They had less material to work on than they wanted, but they consider the comparison to be solid.'

'Come along to my room.'

Seated behind his desk, Tait said, 'We question Harvey again. I'll have a word with Mr Kirby about digging up the concrete.'

'Where do you want to see Harvey, Guv?'

'Here.'

'I suppose he'll have Mr Pascell as nursemaid. Do you intend to charge and arrest him?'

'If you mean Harvey, there's little point in answering at the moment. If you mean Pascell, it would be a pleasure.'

'You don't think Harvey might take a runner when work begins on the concrete?'

'Too self-confident we'll never nail him for her murder ... You'd better start an initial case review for the Crown Prosecution Service.'

'Sir,' Tait said over the phone, 'the lab gives a match between blood on the towel and Mrs Harvey, so I'll put this evidence

before Harvey and find out what explanation he tries to
serve up this time.'

'When?' Kirby asked.

'Later this morning, unless he can give a good reason
otherwise.'

'This afternoon. I'll be down by two so call him in for
two-thirty.'

Tait replaced the receiver. Kirby was determined to present
himself as the key figure in a case which must attract the
attention of the national press.

They were in Interview Room No. 3, noticeably smaller
than the middle one and likely to increase the nervousness
of a suspect with a guilty conscience and a dislike of being
hemmed in.

Pascell said, 'I wish to make it very clear that my client
resents this constant questioning.'

'That is his privilege,' Kirby said. 'Ours is to question
him when we have reason to believe he can help us in our
investigation.'

'He has already answered every question put to him as
fully and as truthfully as he could.'

'You have forgotten his initial answers concerning the
pawning of his wife's engagement ring?' Tait asked.

'Confusion is to be expected when a person is put under
unnecessary pressure.'

'We have asked Mr Harvey to come here,' Kirby said,
'because there is fresh evidence to hand.'

'Concerning what?'

'It will help everyone, Mr Pascell, if you will accept it
is we who are conducting this interview.'

'An unnecessary observation.'

'Mr Harvey, you are aware that during the search
conducted by our officers, a stained towel was found in one
of the two baskets in the bathroom of your house.'

'Yes.'

'It was determined that the stain was human blood. In
view of the fact it lay on top of all the dirty clothing, it is

reasonable to accept it was put in the basket shortly before it was found.'

'We do not accept that,' Pascell said.

'For the moment, we will move on. The nature of the clothing in the basket showed it was used by your wife. We know from Mrs Spens that she would not have put the towel in the basket. Did you?'

'No.'

'Your blood group is A, the blood on the towel was group O. Clearly, the blood had not come from you. A DNA test has been carried out and this established that the blood was from your wife. Do you know what caused her to bleed freely?'

'You have reason to use the word "freely"?'Pascell demanded.

'The towel has been examined by forensic scientists and the description is theirs.'

'Were signs of blood found on the walls or floor?'

'No.'

'In the bath or handbasin?'

'No.'

'Anywhere in the rest of the house?'

'No.'

'Then no more blood was shed than was on the towel.'

'Possibly, Mr Pascell, rather than logically . . . Mr Harvey, was your wife a bleeder?'

'I am uncertain what that means.'

'A person whose blood has slight difficulty in coagulating, rather than the extreme difficulty or impossibility of that of a haemophiliac.'

'I don't think she was.'

'Would she have told you if she had been bleeding too freely from an injury?'

'I doubt it.'

'It would seem to be the normal thing for a wife to do.'

'We had passed the point of exchanging domestic information.'

'Has she appeared to have suffered from any injury? For instance, has she recently been wearing a bandage?'

'No.'

'How do you account for the blood on the towel?'

'I expect she had a nosebleed.'

'Why should you expect that?'

'She was subject to them and they could be prolonged.'

'Did this often happen?'

'Quite frequently.'

'She has consulted a doctor to learn the cause?'

'A long time ago. When she was in her early teens.'

'What was the diagnosis?'

'I don't know.'

'It did not interest you?'

'When I learned of the condition on our honeymoon, I was very worried. All she would say was that it was nothing serious.'

'Do you know which doctor she consulted?'

'No.'

'She has seen no other doctor since then with regard to her complaint?'

'No.'

'You weren't sufficiently worried to suggest that she did?'

'I suggested, she refused.'

'Why do you think she did?'

'She has a fear of doctors.'

'Why?'

'She would never say. I have always thought it was because she is afraid that she would be told she was suffering from something fatal. In matters of her own health, she is an utter pessimist.'

'Then would she not have thought the nose bleeding might be serious?'

'Mr Harvey,' Pascell said, 'has already told you that in her opinion, it was not.'

Kirby spoke to Tait. 'Have you anything to ask, Inspector?'

'I don't think so.'

'Then we will end the interview.'

'It is to be hoped,' Pascell said, as he put papers into his briefcase, 'that you are finally convinced my client has no knowledge as to his wife's present whereabouts.'

'I have carefully listened to all he has said,' was Kirby's reply.

FIFTEEN

The team of PCs, in overalls, waited for the order to commence drilling. Fifty yards away, members of the media complained at their being held back too far from the action. By the road, police tapes had been strung and a PC patrolled to keep the public – already there were several present – at bay.

The air compressor started up and soon its harsh, thumping sound was joined by that of the pneumatic drill. Although the concrete had not had time to mature, it was stronger than expected; men swore.

Tate paced the ground, from time to time glancing at Harvey, who had turned up when the work began. If Harvey understood his crime was soon to be exposed and confirmed, he did not show that fear. A cool customer, Tait thought. Or a life with cows had induced bovinity. As he watched, Harvey walked across to the dairy and went inside.

Tait increased his rate of pacing. They were about to uncover the body of Gillian Harvey, yet still he sought certainty. He wondered yet again with what had Harvey killed his wife? A bolt of wood, baseball bat, crowbar, axe? Yet there had been no blood spatter which seemed to deny those possibilities. The post-mortem should be able to determine the method . . . A file must be prepared to include all statements taken by the police from witnesses, whether these were helpful or unhelpful to the prosecution. The initial report would be sent to the Crown Prosecution Service, later there would be a further review, a senior prosecutor would consider the evidence to decide whether a prosecution was likely to be successful and probably, since the law never moved simply, he would ask for further evidence and clarification of given evidence . . .

His thoughts were interrupted as a PC hurriedly approached him. A message from Kirby, causing trouble?

'Sir . . .' said the PC breathlessly.

'Well?'

'There's a woman who says she's Mrs Harvey. She's demanding to be allowed to pass the barrier.'

'Then do what you should have done and tell her to stop making a nuisance of herself or she'll be arrested.'

'She does look like the photo of Mrs Harvey . . .'

'You have your orders.'

The PC left. Tait resumed pacing. Crime attracted halfwits; occasionally one of whom would even falsely confess. He looked at his watch. How much longer before the men broke through the concrete? Harvey, in the dairy or elsewhere, was surely desperately wondering whether to try to escape before his arrest.

The PC returned. 'Sir . . .'

'Have you got rid of her?'

'No, sir.'

'Why the devil not?'

'She showed me her passport. She is Mrs Gillian Harvey.'

'Don't be a bloody fool.'

'That's what it says, Sir, and it's her photo.'

Tait wondered how the devil a woman could manage to produce Mrs Harvey's passport. The PC seemed incapable of using his common sense. 'It seems I'll have to come and deal with her. When I have, I'll want your sergeant's name.'

He walked across the land and on to the gravel, past the house, and down towards the road. At the tape, a woman was arguing with a PC, gesticulating with the force of anger; the onlookers' attention was on her and no longer on the excavation of the concrete. The passport should not have fooled a fifteen-year-old, Tait mentally told himself. Gillian Harvey was buried beneath the concrete . . .

He came to a stop and people commented on his arrival, misidentifying him. The woman's dress was elegant and of quality; her jewellery was eye-catching; her handbag looked to be of crocodile skin; her resemblance to the photograph which had been circulated around the country was un-mistakable. Even as he asked to see her passport, he began to accept failure.

'Who are you?' she demanded.

'Inspector Tait.'

'I insist you let me enter my property.'

'If I may see your passport?'

She opened her handbag, brought out the passport, thrust it at him. He turned to the identifying details. Gillian Joan Harvey.

'Are you capable of understanding who I am?'

'Yes, Mrs Harvey.' He returned her passport.

'This is outrageous, not being allowed to go into my own home! I shall make the strongest possible complaint.'

It wouldn't matter, his career was already moribund.

She walked to the chauffeur-driven car in which she had arrived and the police tape was drawn aside. Tait walked back to the team who were digging up the concrete and, shouting, told them to stop work. The ugly noise ceased. The sergeant asked him what the problem was.

'The problem is that there is no problem,' he answered bitterly.

SIXTEEN

Kirby, seated in Tait's room at divisional HQ, slammed his fist down on the desk. 'You've made us look like a bunch of brainless idiots. The press are going to have fun ripping us apart.'

'The evidence . . .'

'Evidence? When there hasn't been any, you've invented it. Where there has been, you've twisted it to fit your certainty she was dead. You refused to accept that there might be a natural and normal reason for her disappearance. She was said to be looking forward very much to the arrival of Mrs Ross. She had told Mrs Ross that her marriage was on rocky ground and her husband was always asking for more money, that he thought more of his cows than of her. She did not meet Mrs Ross at the airport, was not at home, left no word of where she had gone. For you, this had to mean she had been unable to make contact because she was dead. To a less committed mind, it would have been obvious that each incident when considered on its own was capable of a simple explanation.'

'The rows were apparently so bitter that when she disappeared, there was reason to . . .'

'Reason only in a mind which refused to consider all possibilities, to a mind which runs along rail tracks. She is rich, he isn't; a prime motive for murder. Never mind that today, many wives are better off than their husbands, but husbands do not rush to murder them. He pawns her engagement ring. He could only have gained possession of it because she was dead. Never a thought to what you were told; that she had been so humiliated by his affair with the Gillmore woman that she no longer wished to wear it. He wanted a feed barn, she refused to fund it. Since he must be a murderer, he had killed her to gain the money to build it.

'She disappears. Because she doesn't draw money from her bank or use her credit cards, she must be dead. Ignore the possibility she has an offshore account she has kept hidden from him. For you, the lack of financial involvement in this country had to be of overwhelming significance.'

'Since there was no hint she did have such an account . . .'

'What clothes were missing? Was her jewellery still in the bank? A towel with her blood on it is in her dirty washing basket. Since she is dead, here is the final proof she has been murdered. Her husband claims she suffers from periodic nosebleeds – of course, he is lying to try and save himself. You reached your judgment at the beginning of the case. When there were two or more possible explanations for something, you chose that which supported your judgment. You've shown blinded misjudgment.'

'It is a pity, Sir, you are accepting so narrow a view.'

'Meaning what?'

'You refuse to accept that while individual circumstances are capable of different interpretations, when there is an interpretation common to all, there is reason for accepting that to be the correct one.'

Neither spoke for a while. The low hum of traffic became noticeable.

'You will question Mrs Harvey,' Kirby finally said, 'and find out why she didn't get in touch with her husband or the police as soon as she heard of her supposed disappearance. If she deliberately refrained from telling anyone, we might be able to find reason to charge her with a waste of police time. That could take some of the flak off us.'

'Why would she have refrained from doing the obvious?'

'To leave her husband under suspicion in order to get her own back for his adultery.'

Gillian Harvey opened the front door of Tanton Farm. 'Yes?' Then she recognized Tait. 'You!' The one word expressed her opinion of him and the rest of the police force.

'I'm very sorry to bother you, Mrs Harvey, but I do have to ask you a question or two.'

'Why?'

'To clear up a slight problem.'

She finally stepped back. He entered, followed her into the sitting room. They sat.

'Please be brief, I have . . .'

She was interrupted when Fiona Ross entered. 'Gil, I wondered . . . Inspector Tait.'

'Good morning, Mrs Ross.'

'Are you here to make your apology on hands and knees?'

'Not exactly.'

'A right plebeian cock-up, we'd call it in Gin Gin.'

'It has all been very unfortunate.'

'A good old Pommy understatement. Well, I'll not hang around in case you accuse me of murdering someone . . . Gil, I'll be back in time to go out for lunch.' She turned and left.

A woman to remember, Tait thought, because of her aggressive self-sufficiency. No circumstance would find her at a loss. 'Mrs Harvey, as I am sure you will understand, we have to draw up a report on what has happened and that must be as complete as we can make it. So would you tell me where you have been for the past weeks?'

'What does that matter?'

'It would help us to know.'

She shrugged her shoulders. 'I've been in Paris.'

'On your own?'

'Yes.'

'Where did you stay?'

'At the hotel where I usually do.'

'While there, did you read or hear about the report that you were supposedly missing?'

'Since I speak French fluently, I watched the local television and read the local papers. There was never any mention of me. The first time I learned I was supposed to have vanished was when I was abruptly denied entry into here.'

'I am sorry about that.'

'The constable called me ridiculous.'

'It was difficult for him . . .'

'Clearly you are all conditioned to believe everyone is a liar.'

There was nothing to be gained from any further apology, but at least he could politely rebuke her. 'All the unpleasantness would have been avoided if Mrs Ross had known why you didn't meet her or were not at home.'

'You think I didn't leave a message for her? That even if I was so desperately upset, I'd forget to tell her where I'd be and suggest she join me?'

'But . . . Are you saying you did leave a message for Mrs Ross?'

'Of course I did.'

'She never received it.'

'As she has told me.'

'Do you know why not?'

'I suffered a very serious nosebleed almost as soon as I arrived in Paris and had to go into hospital. A specialist examined my nose and carried out a minor operation on it. I was desperate to get a message to Mrs Ross and wanted to ring Mrs Spens, but my nostrils were painful and filled with gauze and I was very difficult to understand. So I asked one of the nurses who spoke a very little English to phone Mrs Spens and say where I was so that Mrs Ross would immediately get in touch with me.'

'Mrs Spens didn't tell either your husband or Mrs Ross.'

'She can be a stupid woman.'

'Very stupid.'

'But I imagine you misunderstand her stupidity.'

'In what way?'

'She has an extraordinary, warped hatred of immorality. She suspected my husband's affair and expressed her suspicions to me in fanatical terms. I think her refusal to pass on my message may well have been deliberate and not forgetfulness.'

'I don't quite follow why you should think so.'

'I told the nurse to make the message as simple as possible, just to say I was in Paris. She confessed to having great difficulty in making herself understood and probably Mrs Spens never did understand beyond the fact that the call was coming from Paris. She was young and had an attractive voice. Mrs Spens must have believed she was another girl friend of my husband and therefore was under the messianic obligation to prevent any further meeting.'

Tait didn't express his doubts about what she had said. It all sounded far too complicated and called for Mrs Spens possessing a very convoluted mind. Far more probable, she had forgotten to pass on the message until it had become very late and self-condemning to do so or, having suffered Mrs Harvey's sharp, often ill-tempered and scornful tongue, had deliberately not said anything.

Only one thing was certain. Mrs Spens' silence had resulted in ridiculing the police and damning his career.

Jenner entered Bushell's office.

'You lot again! Then you can tell me what the bleeding hell is going on?' Bushell said pugnaciously. 'I'm so soft, I do a favour and start to lay concrete although I've a dozen more profitable jobs waiting. Then you tell me to stop and my lads are standing around, costing me a fortune. Next thing, you start digging up what had already been laid.'

'It's all rather complicated.'

'Sodding daft.'

'We had to make certain there was not a body under the concrete. Having confirmed there wasn't, there was no need to continue. So now you can replace the concrete and complete the job.'

Bushell swore with little variety. 'I earn an honest living when I'm allowed to. But you lot don't let me because you don't know your asses from your elbows.'

Kirby parked his car behind a couple of others, walked up to the police tape – now unnecessary, but still in place – raised it to pass under, walked across the land to where Tait stood near the concrete base. 'I've had the chief constable on the phone,' he said angrily. 'Told me our incompetence has dragged the force's name through the mud.'

Similar to what Kirby had previously said to him, Tait thought wearily.

'God knows how much money had been wasted by ordering unnecessary work to be done. Had I lost all sense of command . . .'

A pneumatic drill started, overpowering his words. He turned to his left, stared for a moment, spoke when the noise briefly ceased. 'They're digging up, not filling in. What the hell's going on?'

'I'll find out.'

'You should damn well know and I'll do the asking.'

The drilling resumed.

They walked to where Bushell was watching the man drilling at the jagged edges of concrete left from the demolition.

'What are you doing?' Kirby demanded.

Bushell cupped his ear to signify he could not understand. Tait waved his arm to attract the attention of the driller, drew his hand across his throat. All too symbolic, he thought bitterly. The drilling stopped.

'What are you doing?' Kirby demanded again.

'What's it look like?' Bushell replied, equally aggressively.

'You were told to pour concrete, not continue the excavation.'

'You're right, squire, but being stupid enough to want to do a good job, I'm making sure the new surface will bond firmly with the old. Would you like me to explain why that's a good idea?'

Kirby walked away, Tait followed. The drilling resumed.

As soon as the sound was no longer oppressive, Kirby repeated what the chief constable had said to him, demanded to know why Tait had conducted the investigation with all the skill and subtlety of a mind-deranged five-year-old. They reached the car. Kirby opened the passenger door and was about to step in when a man in his early twenties hurried up to them.

'Are you the police?'

Kirby sat, pulled the door shut. 'Yes,' Tait said.

'Morgan, Carnford Courier.'

'There's nothing to tell you.'

'You thought the body of Mrs Harvey was under the concrete?'

'We did not know what was.'

'Then why dig it up?'

'To find out what was there.'

'Was there anything?'

'No.'

'All a load of nonsense then.'

'Circumstances called for the search to be made. The mistake would have been not to make it.'

'What circumstances?'

'Confidential.'

'It's not right then, what people are saying?'

'I've no idea what they are.'

'That you . . .' He stopped as he saw a man running towards them. 'Something up?' he asked hopefully.

The man came to a sharp stop, almost overbalanced and had to gain support from Morgan to save himself from falling. 'There . . . there's a foot under the concrete.'

SEVENTEEN

In some respects, the scene was similar to that of the previous day. Police tape and a PC held the public back, members of the media complained. But it was a team of scene of crime officers in white paper overalls, face masks and security shoes who carried out the excavation.

Photographs and video images were taken as the earth over and around the body was removed with archaeological care. The nature of the soil had delayed decomposition. Her clothes showed she had dressed with little care. She had not been wearing a brassiere; her knickers were torn. Her scuffed trainers were on the point of disintegration. Her eyes were closed, her mouth slightly open and, ironically, her lips might have been about to smile.

The police surgeon, a GP who lived and worked in Carnford, donned protective clothing and examined the body. As required by law, he declared her dead. He did not give the cause of death.

Austin, a Home Office pathologist in protective clothing, spoke to Kirby, stepped down in to the hole and examined the body, taking note of any advice or request from either of the forensic scientists.

It was decided to tape the body. Exposed flesh and clothes were dabbed with strips of Sellotape to pick up contact traces; these strips were placed on transparent sheets for later examination. The body was turned over so that the back could be examined and taped. It was lifted into a body bag, carried to a waiting van and driven to the mortuary.

The ground under and around where the body had lain was examined for insects and their larvae. A key was found, handed up and dropped into an exhibit bag.

Austin climbed out of the hole, removed the protective clothing, which was put into a bag, crossed to where Kirby and Tait waited. 'Do you know who she was?'

'We've no immediate identification,' Tait answered. 'But there is a possibility. From the state of her clothes, rough appearance, and so on, she might be living with the people who call themselves born-again hippies. There's a bunch of them in an abandoned house not very far away and we know Harvey was helped with his cows by one of them from time to time.'

'Any idea of her age?'

'No, but probably fairly young.'

'I'd place the dead woman's age at between twenty-two and thirty. There is evidence of an insect infestation which suggests she was not buried immediately after death. Decomposition gives six to eight weeks since death. Cause of death could be strangulation by hand since there are indeterminate suggestions of bruising on the neck and also on the wrists, which might have been caused by their being held down with considerable force.

'Superficial injuries around the vulva indicate either rape or attempted rape. A possible sequence is she was attacked, held down and her pants ripped as she fought to free herself. Her finger nails were filthy. Their contents will be analysed; judging from the smell, part of it is probably dung.'

'Cow dung?' Tait asked.

'My expertise does not extend that far.'

Kirby, speaking for the first time in a while, said, 'Any foreign hairs?'

'I found none. Closer examination at the p.m. or of the taping may produce some, of course.'

'Any chance of gaining the attacker's DNA?'

'There may be external semen stains, but I saw none. The muck from her nails may produce skin scrapings.'

'When will the p.m. be?'

'Tomorrow morning.'

'Either I or Inspector Tait will be there.'

Austin said goodbye and left with the brisk stride of good health.

'Harvey can provide the identification if the dead woman was his occasional assistant,' Kirby said. 'What has he mentioned about her?'

'Not very much. She was very good with cows and when she did the milking, the yields would be as good as when he did. He reckons she had a lot to do with animals before she turned into a born-again hippy.'

'A farmer's daughter?'

'Or from a wealthy family and she enjoyed playing at being Marie Antoinette.'

'Somewhat far-fetched.'

'Perhaps, sir. But maybe no more far-fetched than voluntarily living in degraded circumstances to show one's rejection of normal standards.'

Tait looked into the CID general room where Miles and Dowling were at work. 'Miles, you can come along with me to take Harvey to the p.m. Down by the car in ten minutes.'

Tait closed the door. Almost immediately, he reopened it and stepped inside. 'Didn't you look for the young woman who from time to time helped Mr Harvey with his cows?'

'Yes, sir. Minnehaha.'

'Then you can identify her?'

'No, sir. When I went to The Grange, she wasn't there and hadn't been for a while.'

'Did you find out where she'd gone or where her home was?'

'I tried, without success. The people there appear and disappear and never talk about their backgrounds.'

'Did you meet any other members of the commune?'

'A woman who said her name was Jane and a man she called Bull.'

'So you'll only be able to identify one other woman from there. Better than none, I suppose, but not by much. Ten minutes, then.' Tait left.

'Been to a p.m. before?' Dowling asked.

'No.'

'The initiation! I bet you'd get out of it if you could?'

'It's part of the job.'

'Sure. But it's bad luck your first should be a woman who's been buried. You know what happens to someone like that?'

'No.'

'The bugs do their work and the juices spill . . . Best not describe any further, though. Don't want to upset you. Do you put perfume on your handkerchief?'

'Of course not.'

'You'll wish you did. It'll stink worse than a bunch of drunken louts in the paddy wagon.'

'Don't they . . .' Miles stopped.

'Waft the scent of violets through the air? When Bones starts ripping, sawing and cutting, he likes to smell because he may pick up the scent of bitter almonds, or whatever. Never stops to think the rest of those present have more sensitive noses.'

Miles' mind began to panic because of what might lie ahead. Dowling laughed.

Tait decided to have a word with Harvey before going on to the hospital mortuary. Fiona Ross opened the front door of Tanton Farm.

'It is true,' she said. 'Like bad pennies, policemen keep turning up.'

'Good morning, Mrs Ross. I've come to ask Mr Harvey to accompany me and identify someone.'

'Judging by the efficiency of you lot, that'll be William Dampier.'

'Events have been far more complicated than they may have seemed to be . . . Is Mr Harvey here?'

'No.'

'Can you suggest where he is?'

'Let me ask the questions. Have you the faintest idea of the emotional upset, the sheer bloody horror you have caused by suggesting Thomas murdered Gillian?'

'Very unfortunately, there are times when we cannot avoid causing distress to others.'

'You've never considered trying to do your job efficiently?'

'Is Mr Harvey working on the farm?'

There was a call from inside the house. 'Who is it, Fiona?'

'Illywhackers.'

'Is Mr Harvey here?' Tait asked again.

'He's gone into town. You'll have to wait to tell him what you've decided it is you'll accuse him of this time.'

'Is Wade here today?'

'I've no idea.'

'We'll go and find out.'

They walked towards the farm buildings. 'Pure bitch!' Tait said bitterly. 'I'll lay ten to one, her ancestors were early arrivals . . . Do you know what an illywhacker is?'

'Not heard the word before, sir,' Miles answered.

'One thing's for sure, it's not complimentary.'

They had almost reached the cowshed when Wade stepped out, stared briefly at them, crossed to the nearest barn and went in.

'Is that Wade?' Tait asked.

'Yes, Sir.'

'You questioned him some time back. Why was that?'

'I was trying to find out who Minnehaha was, Sir.'

'Of course. And he suggested there was something going on between her and Harvey?'

'It was more hints than anything definite. And I did wonder if it was just him trying to make out he knew something to make himself seem important.'

'You think it was all bullshit?'

'Yes, but . . . He did talk with some certainty, I suppose. Like he really had seen Mr Harvey and her together and having a little fun.'

'It would help me if you could decide whether you did or did not believe him.'

They entered the first building and the regular thump of a barley-crushing machine began. Wade was using a screw loader to take barley from the large heap just beyond the crusher up to the feeder on top of it. After a quick glance at them, he stopped the loader and then the machine.

Tait crossed the dusty floor. 'We'd like you to come with us to see if you can identify the victim.'

'Ain't likely.'

'On the contrary. You may have known her, since it is possible she sometimes worked here.'

'You . . . you ain't saying . . .'

'You will be able to confirm whether or not the dead woman is the one who called herself Minnehaha.'

Wade muttered something.

'Are you ready?'

'What for?'

'To find out if you can make an identification.'

'I've work to do.'

'You'll be back before you know you've left.'

Wade brushed himself down, followed them to the car.

They drove on to the road. Tait asked Wade, who sat on the front passenger seat, 'Do you know why she was called Minnehaha?'

'Ain't never heard.'

'As I understand things, she just turned up one day, looking like a hippy, and she helped with the cows.'

'Wasn't like that.'

'Then how was it?'

'Said she wanted to work with the cows. Told her to clear off. Didn't want the likes of her around.'

'But she came here quite often?'

'She kept asking. Didn't get nowhere with me. Then Mr Harvey turns up and she asks him and he says she can.'

'Why was that?'

'Can't rightly say except . . .'

'Well?'

'Seemed to take a liking to her.'

'Did you?'

'Got along with her, that's all.'

'What did you learn about her life?'

'Nothing.'

'Didn't she talk about herself?'

'No. I reckoned she had to come from farming so asked. She wouldn't answer.'

'Then you don't know where she lived before she was at The Grange?'

'That's right.'

'Did you ever think she might have come from a wealthy family?'

'With her living where she did?'

'The way she spoke didn't make you think she might have done?'

'No.'

'We've been told she wore a bracelet which was probably gold.'

'What if she did?'

'That suggests a better background.'

'Wasn't worth nothing. She told me she'd given a quid for it at some boot sale. More likely nicked it.'

Conversation virtually ceased until they parked by the hospital mortuary. Miles, remembering Dowling's description of a post-mortem, suffered an increasing reluctance to leave the car and only did so when Tait wanted to know if he'd fallen asleep.

The mortuary technician led them into the office. In the next fifteen minutes, SOCOs, photographer and forensic scientists joined them. Wade was called into the mortuary chapel to identify the body.

'That's her,' he muttered.

'Will you say her name, please?'

'Only knew her as Minnehaha.'

The post-mortem began. Miles managed to retain his composure until the sounds of the saw on bone.

Having completed his examination of the dead woman, Austin spoke to Tait and Miles in the office.

'The deceased suffered uncompleted strangulation during attempted rape. There is finger bruising on the neck and wrists visible under the skin, as I suggested there might be. However, she did not die from strangulation, but a sudden vagal inhibition, undoubtedly due to the terror of what she was suffering. It would have been obvious to the rapist she had died and that would be the reason why rape was not completed.'

'Death not intended,' Tait muttered, 'but murder all the same.'

'The body had been moved after death. There were grains of barley caught up in it which could suggest it had been concealed in loose barley between death and burial. The material under her nails contained scrapings of flesh and dung. The senior scientist reckons they are unlikely to provide a DNA because of the heavy contamination. It is impossible to give a more accurate time of death and burial than I have said.'

Fifteen minutes later, Tait and Miles left the building and crossed to their car; Wade said he wanted to buy something in town and would return to the farm on the bus. Tait opened the driving door, looked across the roof. 'Are you all right, Miles? Your first p.m.? You'll soon get used to it.'

Miles gained no relief from that assurance.

The key found under the body was returned from the laboratory with the advice that nothing of significance was found on it. Jenner was ordered to take it to the farm and find out if there was a lock on any of the buildings which it would open. Success was quick. It fitted the door of the office in the cowshed.

He returned to the station and reported to Tyler.

'Did you check the key in any of the other locks you had not already tried?'

'Wouldn't work any of 'em.'

Jenner left. Tyler put the key back in the exhibit bag in which it had arrived. In his mind, he constructed the probable sequence of events. Wade's evidence showed that Harvey had accepted Minnehaha on the farm when one might well have expected him to echo Wade's attitude and tell her to clear off. Why hadn't he? He could not have known then whether she had any knowledge of, or ability with, animals. One answer was obvious. Wade had indicated Harvey had been attracted to Minnehaha. She had died while the attempt was made to rape her. By law, this was murder.

Unable to think logically in the face of this catastrophe, Harvey had buried the body under the loose barley by the crusher. After a while, he had been able to think logically once more. Concrete would provide the best possible hiding place so he had to make certain work on the base began very quickly. He had dug out more earth, prepared to tip the body into the extra space when, unknown to him, his key had fallen from his pocket into the hole. He had used excavated earth to tamp that down over the body. Concreting had begun. His crime would not have become apparent if Mrs Ross had not insisted something had happened to Mrs Harvey . . .

EIGHTEEN

Tait completed his report to Kirby over the phone. 'That's the score, sir.'

'What steps are you taking to trace her family?'

'The mortuary technician will smooth out her face so it can be photographed. We'll ask for the media's help in publicizing the request for identification. Since we've no idea which region of the country she may have come from, I see no practical reason at the moment to send out fliers.'

'You are not attempting to find direct evidence?'

'Of course we are, sir, but it's very doubtful we will be successful.'

'It is not a good idea to start by accepting failure. Have you questioned Harvey further?'

'No, since I'm only just back from the p.m.'

'What about the man who does occasional work? He may know something about her.'

'He does not seem to be able to help, but he'll be questioned again this afternoon . . . You will remember, sir, that he indicated Harvey and Minnehaha . . .'

'Must you use that ridiculous name?'

'It's the only one we have, sir.' He waited, continued. 'Previously, when Miles was talking to him, he indicated Harvey was either having, or trying to have, an affair with Minn . . . the girl. That suggests . . .'

'From now on, you'll conduct this investigation without endless assumptions and presumptions. Facts, Tait, only unquestioned facts. Facts that can be proven, that lead to the truth, not imaginative nonsense. Is that clear?'

'Yes, sir.'

'You'll be lucky if you're only returned to uniform if you make the force a laughing stock for the second time.'

'That's not going to happen, since the girl is dead.'

'Given half a bloody chance, you'll discover she's still alive.' Kirby rang off.

Tait swore. Kirby had accepted, even encouraged the assumption that surrounding circumstances had confirmed Gillian Harvey was dead. But seniority ensured only those lower down the ladder were drenched by the contents of the slop pail.

Miles drove into the grounds of The Grange. The discarded tins and bottles had increased in number, the flag of unwelcome was too tattered to be legible and more of the windows of the house had been broken which in August was of small moment, but in December might suggest to those trying to keep warm the stupidity of wanton destruction. The guttering, which had been hanging, was on the ground, the mural had been disfigured with more sprayed paint to become a meaningless hotchpotch of colour. Half the front door now lay on the floor.

He stepped into the hall. The damaged marble floor remained littered with empty cans and someone in the near past had been sick on it. Two men, who stood by the staircase, smoking, stared belligerently at him.

'Afternoon,' he said.

There was no reply.

'I'm looking for Jane.'

The elder man, whose shirt looked as if it had been used in a vain attempt to clean the floor, hawked and spat.

'Do you know where she is?'

'No.'

'Would you find her for me?'

'You reckon I'm a pimp.'

'I merely wish to speak to her.'

They continued to stare at him.

He walked into the room on his right. A couple were smoking pot. In the next room, four women and two men were listening to Mozart's *Don Giovanni*, the music almost ruined by the poor reproduction. The kitchen had equipment, mostly broken, which dated back many years.

In an upstairs bedroom, Jane and Bull lay on a stained mattress.

'Shit,' she exclaimed.

'You know him?' Bull asked.

'So do you. He's fuzz.'

'What d'you want?' Bull demanded.

'A chat with Jane,' Miles replied.

'How d'you know her name?'

'She told me.'

'Are you bleeding mad?' Bull shouted at Jane.

'What's it matter if he does know it? All he's interested in is saving souls. Wants to look good when he's judged.'

'He's been nicking things?'

'It's his soul, you berk.' She turned to Miles. 'What's it this time? You've decided to try and have some nookie?'

Bull spoke violently. 'He touches you and I'll kill the bastard.'

'You're being real sharp, threatening to kill a copper. If they can ever find your IQ, it'll be negative.' She stood, picked up a pair of pants and drew them up under her frock as she said to Miles, 'What's to chat about?'

'I'll tell you outside.'

She hesitated, finally moved and walked out of the room ahead of him. They went down the back stairs and out through a side door into sunshine.

She came to a halt by a small pile of smashed bottles.

'I thought you wouldn't let Bull touch you,' Miles said.

'What's it to you?'

'Nothing.'

'Jealous?'

'No.'

'Ain't no law against it, is there?'

'I hope not. Have you heard about Minnehaha?'

'Gone back to her darling mummy?'

'I'm afraid she's dead.'

'Happens to everyone.'

'Murdered.'

She stared at him, murmured, 'Christ!', and sat on the

grass without bothering to make certain it was clear of glass.

A swallow flew over them in a curving swoop and landed on a nest built under a length of guttering which still stood. 'And the swallow a nest where she may lay her young' unexpectedly came to his mind, but he couldn't remember where he had learned that or where it came from. He sat by her side after checking the ground was clear of rubble.

'I kept saying . . .' She stopped.

'What?'

'But she wouldn't.' She was speaking to herself, not to him. 'Wouldn't clear out. Couldn't understand. We want to live this life, she only thought she did . . . She had somewhere to go back to.'

'What makes you think that?'

'Because she was forever going off to the cows. They meant something special to her. And she was always trying to escape drugs, drunks and groping hands. When talk was dirty, she joined in, but it didn't come easy to her. She wanted to belong, but couldn't.'

'You're saying she came from a good background?'

'I suppose.'

'You don't know where her home was?'

'She never said.'

'And you weren't curious enough to try and find out?'

She picked a piece of grass and began to chew the end of it. 'What's it matter now?'

'It would help lessen the tragedy if we could identify her parents or relations.'

'When you tell 'em she's been murdered?'

'It would at least end their pain of not knowing whether or not she's still alive.'

'They're maybe like mine. Don't give a shit.'

'Of course they worry about you.'

'Never had to endure a drunken father and a stepmother who hates you? . . . How was she killed?'

'During an attempted rape.'

'God, what a way to go!' There was a long pause. 'Where did you find her?'

'Under newly laid concrete at the farm.'

'What's she ever done to end up like that? . . . She used to sing. Did you know?'

'No.'

'Soft, sentimental. They jeered at her because it wasn't cool. Then Steve backed her with his guitar and there was no more jeering. But they didn't want to do it again. Dug too deep into memories.' She spat out the grass. 'No good asking for a joint, I suppose?'

'Hopeless.'

'Got a fag?'

'I don't smoke.'

'Only have to look at you to know it was a stupid question . . . Who killed her?'

'We don't yet know.'

'Got to be one of them at the farm.'

'Why?'

'Who else?'

'Someone here?'

'They didn't like her, but kind of respected her.'

'Would that stop one of them?'

'Why bother to go to the farm to try to rape her when she was here most of the time?'

He didn't try to answer.

'You've got to get the bastard.'

'We will. I suppose she often talked about the farm?'

'If you could be bothered to listen.'

'Did she mention Mr Harvey?'

'Said he knew more about cows than Bull did about women.'

'Did she like him?'

'He was fun until he went on at her to pack it in here and return home.'

'So there were several people trying to persuade her.'

'There was something about her . . . When she disappeared, I thought she'd come to her senses and returned home. Kind of made me happy, even though I hated her for having the chance. Didn't dream she'd been . . . What a sodding, filthy world this is.'

'Do you think there was anything between her and Mr Harvey?'

'What's it to you? Wish you'd enjoyed it first?'

'Hardly, when I had to look at her dead body.'

After a while, she muttered, 'Sorry.'

'I'm asking because you could be able to help nail her killer.'

'You think it was Harvey?'

'We've no reason to believe who it was. We just need to learn all we can about her life.'

'I could help?'

'Yes.'

'She was certain Harvey must be hot because his wife had shut her bed, but she never said he'd been trying to get into her pants.'

'Did she ever talk about a particular part of England, Wales or Scotland which might suggest where her home was?'

'No.'

'Why was she called Minnehaha?'

'When Arnie was here – thought himself real sharp – he hated her because he understood she wasn't the shit he was. They had an argument which got real hard because for once she didn't just lie down. In the end, she showed him a map and said it proved she was right and it was that high. He lost his temper and gave her a clout, she started crying and that's when he called her Minnehaha.'

'What was the argument about?'

'Can't remember. Likely it was nothing. Arnie thought he knew everything and couldn't take being told he was wrong.'

'What area did the map show?'

'Somewhere up north.'

'You can't be more specific?'

'No.'

'What was she originally called?'

'Something like Judy. Or was it Janet? I don't know. Maybe it was Susan.'

'I've been told she used to wear an attractive bracelet.'

'It didn't do anything for me.'

'But it was valuable?'

'Are you moon walking? If that had been valuable, it would have been nicked by someone. Probably Bull, so he could snort some more. Like she said, she bought it at a junk stall because it looked fun. What gets you interested?'

'The bracelet wasn't with her body. I suppose she didn't wear it all the time?'

'Yes, she did. Told her it was stupid because even if it was only worth a couple of quid, that would buy some booze for whoever nicked it. She never listened.'

'Was she wearing it before she disappeared?'

'I expect so.'

'You can't be certain?'

'Look, mister, I don't worry about what people wear. All I know is, I never saw her without it. You want to know something? I think it meant much more to her than just a bracelet.'

'You're now saying what?'

'I don't know what I'm saying.'

'Fair enough. I'd be grateful if you'd take me to where she kept her things.'

He thought she was going to refuse, then she stood and led him up to the bedroom next to the one in which she had been earlier. Against one wall, on a tattered sheet on a mattress which had probably been discarded by the previous owner, was a dishevelled clutter of clothes on top of which was a book in a brown-paper cover. He picked up the book and opened it. Life in a manor house in the nineteenth century. Had the brown paper cover been camouflage to prevent further contempt for her tastes and, by inference, her background? He heaped the clothes, two blankets and a pillow, all in dire need of cleaning, on the sheet. Under the pillow was a small teddy bear, its coat almost worn away by constant handling. Memory of childhood innocence? 'I'll be away.'

'Nothing more you want?'

'I don't think so.'

'I can't give you something?'

'Very kind of you, but no.'

He left, uneasily wondering whether if he had accepted her invitation, he would have helped her through the emotional stress from the knowledge of the murder.

NINETEEN

Tyler looked up as Miles entered his room.

'I've had a chat with Jane at The Grange, Sarge.'

'So my watch tells me. What it doesn't add is, who is Jane?'

'The young lady I met the last time I was there.'

'Lady, as on the streets.'

'She may be leading a rough life, but that's because life has been kicking her since she was born.'

'Kicks everyone whose name isn't Gates.'

'Her father's a drunk and her stepmother hates her.'

'And her uncle was torn apart when he was crossing Tower Bridge and it opened. Wake up, lad. She was after a couple of quid from you so she could buy a stick.'

'I'm sure that was the truth.'

'With your trusting soul, you'd pay heavy for a letter from the Pope congratulating Henry on his marriage to Anne Boleyn. I suppose you were too sympathetic to her misery to remember why you were there?'

'There was never any suggestion Minnehaha was having it off with Harvey.'

'Just forgot to mention what was going on between milking the cows. His spoilsport of a wife might become suspicious, so Minnehaha had to go.'

'I can't see Mr Harvey trying to rape her.'

'Not noticed his wrists?'

'What about them?'

'If at the morgue you hadn't been like a maiden aunt seeing her first cherry-splitter, you'd have noticed the small scars on one of his wrists. Since she dug her fingers into the arms of whoever was on top of her, they talk.'

'But . . .'

'Likely Dowling can persuade Wade to tell him about when they were milking each other instead of the cows.'

Dowling knocked on the front door of Perce Hall. After a moment, a panel in the door was opened. 'Who is it?'

'Constable Dowling, county police.'

The panel was shut and the door was opened by Mrs Wade, in a wheelchair. He wished her good afternoon, explained he wanted a word with her husband.

'On account of that poor woman?'

'Sadly, yes.'

'Not safe anywhere these days. Ted put the chain on the door and said I was to fix it whenever he was out.'

'Very wise, Mrs Wade. Is he here?'

'I wouldn't be opening the door if he was. I tell him, when he's around to do the work, I'm sitting.' She smiled.

'Would you know where he is right now?'

'Butler's Farm. Been all day as they're harvesting.'

'How do I get to there?'

'Take the road to Prestley and turn right at the signpost to Carnford. It's half a mile along.'

Ten minutes' driving along lanes, at one point canopied by the heavy branches of ancient oaks on either side, and he came to Butler's Farm. In a ten-acre field, wheat was being harvested by a combine. Wade was loading sacks on to a tractor's trailer. Dowling crossed and spoke to him, shouting to overcome the noise.

'I'll have to tell the boss.'

'Do that.'

Dowling retired to the edge of the field. His father had been a farmer and his comments about the old days had been interesting until they became boring. Rabbits held at bay by the circling harvester until the last remaining lines of standing corn, then bolting to be shot by waiting guns. The jeers if a fleeing rabbit, unable to run at full speed on the stubble, was missed . . .

Wade came to where he stood. 'He says keep it short.'

'Will do. Shall we sit?'

There was a small bank in front of the hedge and this

afforded just enough room on which to settle. 'I reckon you're here on account of her?' Wade said.

'That's right.'

'Nasty, her being killed like that.'

'Very nasty.'

'Thought she'd just wandered off, like she'd wandered in. Then you lot thought it was Mrs Harvey what was missing.'

'We can all make mistakes. Some time ago, you suggested Mr Harvey was friendly with Minnehaha? More than friendly?'

'How d'you mean?'

Dowling spoke with jovial, suggestive interest. 'Did you see 'em kissing?'

'Maybe.'

'Nice-to-see-you-again kissing or it's-time-to-lie-down?'

'Ain't right to say.'

'Why not?'

'Ain't for talking about.'

'It is when she was found throttled and buried under concrete after having been stored somewhere.'

'She wasn't buried immediate?'

'So the experts say. Now, if we're to find out who the bastard was, we need you to tell us what you know. How ardent was the kissing?'

'Don't reckon it could have got more.'

'Did he give her a tickle on the Bristols or a pat on the bum to tell how much he appreciated her bits and pieces?'

'Might have done.'

'You're as full of information as my grandfather and he died years back. What about putting his hand under her skirt?'

'She wore trousers.'

'Women will do anything to make life difficult. Have you ever seen them playing daddy and mummy?'

'Maybe.'

'Tell me about it.'

'Don't seem right speaking.'

'We've been through all that, so let's be hearing.'

'Told him I wouldn't be along because there was work in the next village. There wasn't any, so I came here on account of there always being something to do. Looked to find him to say what he wanted and went to the office.'

'Was the door locked?'

'Can't say.'

'Why not?'

'Didn't try to open it on account of what was going on inside.'

'How did you know what was without opening the door?'

'Heard her telling him she didn't want to. He said as she was having it every night at the commune so why be difficult?'

'And?'

'She kept saying she wasn't having any. He offered her a fiver.'

'Hardly generous. What was her response?'

'Wasn't none until she told him to stop.'

'Did he?'

'Can't say. Didn't like hearing, so left.'

'How often did you hear or see them having fun?'

'Only then.'

'Is there anything more you can tell me about their amusements?'

'Said too much already.'

Tait said, 'He was trying to screw her in his office in the cowshed. Then there's reason to suppose he failed, tried again days later and that's when he killed her. Tell SOCO to go over the office with a fine-tooth comb.'

Dowling, standing in front of the desk, said, 'Wouldn't their usual kit be more useful?'

'If there's one thing starts me thinking a man doesn't fit his job, it's when he tries to be a comedian.'

Dowling left.

Tait rang county HQ, spoke to Kirby, and gave his report. 'If the wife had learned, she'd have kicked him out of home, so he had to do something fast.'

'She knew he was humping Mrs Gillmore, but hadn't got rid of him.'

'This would have caused a much greater uproar, because Minnehaha . . . The dead girl lived in a commune. Mrs Harvey would have seen that as a double insult. At least Mrs Gillmore is very presentable.'

'You reckon Mrs Harvey doesn't know about this second affair?'

'Not even a hint about it. So it'll be kind to keep her ignorant until it has to come out in court.'

'When a man shops around, he must expect to have to pay the price.'

At training college, Kirby had been an eager shopper. 'It seems feasible he murdered her in the office in the cowshed. I've called for SOCO to examine the room for traces.'

'Why hasn't that been done before?'

'The farm offers so many places for murder, it seemed impractical to carry out a full forensic search until a probable, or even possible, location could be named.'

'You took that decision on your own account?'

'No, sir. With the advice of SOCO,' Tait replied, with satisfaction.

TWENTY

Dowling parked in front of the farmhouse, switched off the engine, did not immediately move. That morning, Laura had told him she was pregnant. After the hints he had been receiving, he should not have been surprised by the information, but still he had been and that had been obvious. Laura, normally so sensible, had imagined his emotion was not surprise, but bitter annoyance, and she had become almost hysterical. Did he want her to have an abortion, was he going to throw her out and find someone who wasn't big bellied, perhaps he'd try to claim he wasn't the father . . . It had taken a long time to persuade her that he had always wanted a son who'd play rugger for England or a daughter who'd win The Horse of the Year Show. She had hugged him and tearfully admitted she had been unforgivably stupid. It would, he decided, be sensible to buy some flowers before he returned home.

He finally left the car, crossed to the front door and knocked. Mrs Spens opened it. Surprise, minor key, assailed him again. 'You're back!'

'And why shouldn't I be?' she demanded.

'You said you couldn't stay in the house when Mr Harvey . . .'

'I had to leave for a short while because of a friend's illness. It had nothing to do with Mr Harvey. I knew it couldn't be true what people were saying and when someone asked me how could I bear to stay on here with him, I told her what I thought of her and the rest of them.'

'Good to hear that. I hope your friend is better?'

She did not answer.

'You being here saves me from asking Mr or Mrs Harvey for your address.'

'Why did you want that?'

'To ask you a question or two. May I come in?'

As he stepped into the hall, there was a call from one of the rooms. 'Who is it?'

Mrs Spens crossed to a half-open door. 'A policeman, Mrs Harvey.'

'Not again!'

'Just like home,' Fiona Ross said loudly, as she joined in the conversation. 'Always around when you don't need one. What does he want?'

'To ask me something.'

'Tell him to be quick and leave.'

'Best come into the kitchen,' Mrs Spens said to Dowling.

His failure to refute her earlier lies had clearly softened her manner. In the kitchen, she offered him coffee.

'Yes, I would like some, please.'

'Then sit and I'll make it for the both of us.'

Despite the command to be brief and return to the station as soon as possible, it was not before he had drunk two cups of coffee and eaten three chocolate biscuits that he said he'd like to ask her a few questions concerning 'the poor woman' who had been murdered.

She declared her opinion of females who lived in sin, looked like tramps, refused to work, swindled the social services, begged and stole.

'She was kind in the way she helped Mr Harvey and he reckons she was a very good cowman, or cowwoman,' he observed.

'So I've heard him say.'

'Did you know her well?'

'Of course not.'

'But you must have had many a chat with her?'

'Only when she was in the house and I had to say something.'

'She often came here?'

'Mr Harvey chose to have her for coffee and sometimes even a drink,' she said with sharp condemnation.

'Then he must have got on well with her?'

'Said he was sorry for her. There's no reason to feel sorry for the likes of her.'

'She must have led a very different kind of life from him. And usually, I don't suppose there would have been a friendship. I wonder . . . Do you imagine there could have been a reason for that friendship which had nothing to do with cows?'

'Can't say.'

'I'm afraid I'll have to ask you something you will find very objectionable to answer. Did you ever see them behave in a way which made you think perhaps their relationship went beyond work?'

He thought she was going to refuse to answer. Then, tight-lipped, she said, 'Why else would he have her in the sitting room?'

'You think that was . . . significant?'

'He can shut the door, can't he? It only happened when Mrs Harvey was out. He knew what Mrs Harvey would say if she found that slut in the house.'

'She might suspect her husband was having another affair?'

There was silence.

'Do you think that was likely?'

'I don't think such things.'

'Even though Mr Harvey only had Mrs Gillmore in the house when Mrs Harvey was away?'

'I do not jump to immoral conclusions.'

Just as she had never believed the rumours, he thought.

Miles separated from Irene as they heard the front door of her house open. She adjusted her clothes.

'Evening, Eric,' Ramsey said, as he entered the sitting room, followed by his wife. 'How's life? The dragon still breathing fire?'

'Never does anything else, likely because his boss is always on at him.'

'Big fleas have little fleas on their backs to bite 'em.'

'Great fleas,' corrected Beatrice, his wife.

'The benefit of being married to an erudite wife!'

Miles smiled. The Ramseys often sparred verbally, always without rancour.

Once seated, Beatrice said, 'I want to know if you two have any firm ideas yet about when to have the wedding?'

'We were discussing that just before you came in, Mum,' Irene answered. 'We've been wondering about the end of September.'

'We'll have a chat later, but right now that sounds fine. I'd better go through and get the meal ready. You've prepared the beans and potatoes?'

'I . . . Sorry, mum.'

'More interesting things to do?' Ramsey asked archly. 'Now, which of the three reasons for drinking shall we favour?'

'Five reasons,' Beatrice corrected.

'The more the merrier. There's lager for the boys, Guinness for the men, gnat's pee sherry for the ladies.'

'I wish you wouldn't say that.'

Ninety minutes later, they had finished their meal and returned to the sitting room where they drank coffee, except for Beatrice who preferred hot chocolate.

'Are you any nearer catching the bloke who murdered the girl?' Ramsey asked.

'You know you're not to ask him about his job,' Beatrice said reprovingly.

'I'm not asking who, just if.'

'And he's not going to answer you.'

Miles spoke to Beatrice, whom he had not yet learned to call by her Christian name even though she had suggested he did. 'I wonder if you could tell me something, Mrs Ramsey?'

'An insulting question,' Ramsey observed 'since you're obviously assuming she might not be able to.'

There was brief laughter.

'What's the question?' Beatrice asked.

'Is there any particular reason for calling someone Minnehaha?'

'Because she's female?' Ramsey suggested.

'Why are you asking, Eric? These days, parents call their children the most extraordinary names and never stop to think how these will affect their children when at school and the others mock them.'

'A man gave a woman this nickname after an argument.'

'Then it was intended to be derisive?'

'Almost certainly.'

'Minnehaha was Hiawatha's bride.'

'Explains everything,' Ramsey said sardonically.

She spoke to Miles. 'Did this woman have a boyfriend who annoyed her because he decided to call himself Hiawatha?'

'I don't think so.'

'Then I can't help except to say that at school we had to study Longfellow's *Hiawatha* and, if I remember correctly, Minnehaha meant waterfall or laughing water in Sioux.'

Had the argument between Minnehaha and Arnie been over the situation of a river? Miles tried to remember exactly what Jane had said. Height had been mentioned? Rivers didn't have height in the normal sense . . . But certainly waterfalls did.

TWENTY-ONE

'I think I learned something which could be important from Jane last night, Sarge,' Miles said.

Tyler nodded as he continued to read the latest memorandum from HQ. It was to be noted that in the judgment in Regina v Peterson, it was held that a shutter was not a window. Clever men, lawyers.

Miles coughed, then coughed again.

Tyler looked up. 'Try honey and lemon.'

'Sarge, I may have found out why Minnehaha was called what she was.'

'Fascinating. Now, give your brain a rest and do some work.'

'I feel right sorry for Jane.'

'So you've said before.'

'But to suffer parents like hers.'

'What did she end up by taking you for? A couple of quid?'

'She wasn't asking for anything. Quite the contrary.'

'She was offering?'

'Yes.'

'Then it's to be hoped you didn't end up with more than you expected.'

'According to Jane, Minnehaha had a sharp argument with a bloke called Arnie about where something was and its height and she proved herself right with a map. This so annoyed Arnie, he called her Minnehaha in derision. In the Sioux language . . .'

'I've got the Guv'nor screaming and you want to tell me how the Sioux said, "Good morning, how are you?"'

'The name means laughing water or waterfall.'

'Will it disturb you to know that I don't give a toss if it means apples are ten pence a pound?'

'But like I said, she showed Arnie a map and proved

herself right and that so pissed him off, he made fun of her and called her Minnehaha. What if it was an argument over waterfalls and she knew the answer when he didn't? What if the map of somewhere up north detailed a waterfall and gave its height? Why would she have such a map and know about the waterfall? Because she had lived in that area and the map was a sentimental reminder? Was there a nearby waterfall? I've checked and the highest waterfall in England is on the Tees. If one chooses an area around there and puts up fliers asking for an identification, her parents might see one. They could be told what had happened and however sad that would make them, they'd no longer have to wonder if she was alive or dead . . . What do you think?'

'Right now, I can't decide whether you've been wasting your time or doing something useful.'

Tait answered the phone.

'I can't be with you at eleven and I don't yet know when I'll be free,' Kirby said.

'Then I'll question Harvey about his relationship with the woman, sir.'

'You'll wait until I'm with you.'

The call ended.

Tyler looked out of the window as he scratched his nose, which itched when it was going to rain heavily – it was a sunny day. A summer to be remembered, since it had lasted more than a week. His wife was a sun lover. Whenever it had been sunny and he was free, she had organized a picnic down by the sea. She would wear her reduced bikini, which he would have enjoyed seeing on another woman, but not on his wife. Did she take her lover down to the sea for a picnic? If so, did she briefly, unwillingly, remember the times she had been with him . . .?

The phone interrupted his thoughts. For a moment, he stared at it as he accepted the stupidity of conjuring up bitter memories and questions, then lifted the receiver.

'Constable Elliot, SOCO. Re: Tanton Farm. We found

traces in the office in the cowshed which are human and suggest sudden death. The lab will try to extract DNA from them, but can't say what's the chance of success.'

Tyler went along to Tait's office. It was empty. He wrote a brief note, left this in the centre of the desk. He wondered if Harvey had any inkling of how freedom was deserting him at an ever-increasing speed.

Kirby arrived at divisional HQ at eight-ten, Tait at eight-fifteen.

'I expect my officers to respect the demands of their work,' was Kirby's greeting.

'I had difficulty in starting the car, sir.'

'You do not consider it advisable to allow for such eventualities by leaving earlier?'

Tait allowed himself a small measure of disrespect. 'As you once said at the training college when you arrived twenty minutes late for a lecture because of the press of traffic, since it is impossible to allow for every conceivable adverse eventuality, there is not much point in choosing which one to consider.'

'I have no memory of the incident. Are you finally ready?'

They hardly spoke on their drive to Tanton Farm.

Mrs Spens told them Mr Harvey was upstairs having a bath after milking and breakfast and they must wait in the sitting room until he was ready to speak to them. Kirby was annoyed by her manner.

Harvey entered the room twenty minutes later. 'Sorry to keep you waiting.'

'And we're sorry to bother you again,' Kirby answered.

So it was going to begin softly, softly, Tait thought. The detective chief superintendent must find that difficult.

Harvey sat. 'I'd be grateful if you could be as quick as possible. I've rather a lot to do today.'

'I think I can say, we're only just tidying up. Some of the questions will have been put to you before, but please bear with me. Am I right in thinking you have no recollection of any intruder on the farm shortly before . . .' He paused; finally said, 'Before Minnehaha disappeared?'

'I saw no one.'

'I imagine you suffer people trespassing?'

'In the summer, we often find picnickers in one of the fields down to hay or silage. They seem unable to understand why that should annoy us.'

'How do you deal with them?'

'I ask them as politely as I can manage to leave. If Wade is doing the asking, he tells them to bugger off.'

'Do they ever come up as far as the sheds?'

'Not that I can ever remember.'

'Perhaps that's surprising when Mr Joe Public is told that in the days of equality he has the right to go anywhere. I suppose, in case there should be unwanted visitors, you keep the office in the cowshed locked?'

'Yes.'

'All the time?'

'Yes.'

'How many keys are there?'

'That's an odd question.'

'Nevertheless, perhaps you'll answer it.'

'Three, I think.'

'You can't be certain.'

'Call it three.'

'Does anyone else have the right and ability to enter the office?'

'Fred, when I ask him to.'

'And did the dead woman?'

'Yes.'

'Did she have a key?'

'When, as with Fred, she'd come to me and ask for mine.'

'Why would she want to go in there?'

'To record the individual yields after milking.'

'Was she often around?'

'Sometimes frequently; sometimes there would be days before she turned up again.'

'Did you know her well?'

'In a working sense, yes. In a personal sense, no. She was very secretive about herself.'

'Did you like her?'

'I found her attitude to living disturbing. Tomorrow didn't exist until tomorrow so it was never tomorrow.'

'Ignoring that side of her.'

'She was interesting and quite often amusing.'

'You didn't mind the fact she was in a commune?'

'We worked together, laughed together, and when something went wrong, she cursed a sight more fluently than I.'

'Did you ever see her when away from the cows?'

'No.'

'You didn't ever invite her up to the house for a coffee?'

'Sorry, I thought you meant away from the farm. Yes, from time to time, much to Mrs Spens' disapproval.' He laughed. 'Mrs Spens has very firm rules about social boundaries.'

'Did Wade join you?'

'No. He's a solid worker, but not a good social companion.'

'Did your wife like the girl?'

'Gillian disapproved of her mode of life, her dress, her manners. That may not cover all her dislikes.'

'Yet she welcomed your having the girl in for a coffee?'

'I made a point of not inviting Minnehaha if Gillian was at home. No point in courting trouble.'

'Did you know there had been an attempt to rape the girl before she died suddenly?'

'Christ! No, I didn't.'

'We think she was buried some time after she was murdered. That means her body was hidden almost certainly somewhere around the farm. Would you say it would be easy to hide a body here?'

'I suppose it wouldn't be difficult for a short time.'

'Why only that?'

'It would start to stink.'

'No offence, Mr Harvey, but as a townsperson, I find there is a constant smell around here.'

'You think the smell of dung would be overriding? I doubt that.'

'Her clothing and body had several grains of barley in them. Does that suggest anything to you?'

'No.'

'I believe there is a large amount of barley by the crusher in the shed?'

'In the home-made silo? That's only full when the barley's just been delivered. The rest of the time, I'm hoping the barley will last until the next load is due to be delivered.'

'Could the body have been buried in the grain?'

'My God! What a question!'

'Would that be possible?'

'The depth of grain would be sufficient some of the time, I suppose. But even allowing for the smell of the cows . . .'

'Decomposition may well not reach that point for two to four days. I imagine you had no reason to search the contents of the silo?'

'None at all.'

'Previously, you've mentioned Minnehaha wore a bracelet and you told her you thought it rather silly to do so. Why?'

'I reckoned it was probably too valuable to flourish in the commune, but she told me it was only cheap imitation.'

'You did not believe her?'

'It was gold.'

'Why are you so certain? She showed you the marks?'

'No. But it became daubed over and over again in muck and never lost its colour, never showed any tarnishing. I doubt anything but gold could put up with that treatment and remain bright.'

'How would you describe the bracelet?'

'Difficult. The best I can do is two strips wound spirally around each other which ended in engraved heads.'

'Heads of what?'

'Could have been anything, but she said they were rams' heads.'

'You obviously took quite an interest in it.'

'I was intrigued and was convinced it was ancient, even though she swore it wasn't. I guessed she'd inherited it.'

'Bringing one back to a comfortable background . . . I think we've covered everything, so we'll leave you in peace.

Not, I imagine, that there is much peace where cows are concerned.'

'Rearing babies must be easier.'

Kirby and Tait said goodbye, left.

Kirby did not speak until they were driving up the road. 'If forensics can give us a DNA match, we'll have him fair and square. Facts, facts, that's what we need and that's what we have this time. Facts lead to truth, assumptions to bloody silly mistakes.'

A cock pheasant, a flying rainbow, rose from the grass verge. Tait raised an imaginary twelve bore and fired. The pheasant had had Kirby's head.

Helen hurried into the room. 'What happened? Was he beastly?'

'Surprisingly pleasant,' Harvey answered.

'What did they want?'

'This and that. Did you offer me a drink?'

'No. But you can go and get one for me as well as yourself.'

She sat, he went into the kitchen where he poured out a whisky and a Dubonnet.

'Now you're going to tell me,' she said as he returned.

'They asked questions, I answered them. Let's forget about it.'

'When you are so obviously worried? Please, I must know.'

'What worries me is that the detective superintendent was pleasant. Yet until now, he's been all aggression. Why the change?'

'Because he's no longer stupid enough to imagine you know anything.'

'Maybe. But then there was a hint, maybe more than a hint, that they thought I killed Minnehaha.'

'That would be even more insane than thinking you murdered Gillian. Why in the hell would you hurt the girl when she was so helpful on the farm?'

'There was an attempt to rape her.'

'And you imagine he could think you could be guilty of that? He'd have to be certifiable to believe that.'

TWENTY-TWO

September clouds, wind, and rain spoke of winter in a hurry. The windows of the CID room carried wobbly streaks of rainwater which muddled images beyond.

'What a bloody awful day,' Dowling remarked.

'I've a cousin who lives in Cyprus,' Jenner said.

'So you keep telling us.'

'He rang up for a chat last night. They're enjoying hot sunshine and the sea's like a warm bath.'

'Add he's just won the lottery and you'll make our day.'

'He did win five thousand on the Premium Bonds not long back.'

'It's people like him who destroy one's faith in justice.'

The phone with a long lead had been left on the table by the noticeboard. It rang. After the fourth ring, Jenner said, 'Is everyone deaf?'

They looked at Miles. He stood, accepting he would remain dogsbody until someone with less experience than he joined the team. He answered the call.

'Stitchworth Forensic. We've a match with the DNA of the dead woman, identified as Minnehaha, and the stains on the floor in the office at Tanton Farm. Due to heavy contamination, the very small pieces of skin under the victim's nails could tell us nothing. That's it.'

'You'll be sending an official report?'

'Thank you so much for reminding me what to do.'

Fail to confirm and you were sworn at, Miles thought as he replaced the receiver, confirm and you were sworn at.

'Anything of interest?' Jenner asked.

'The lab says the stains in the office came from Minnehaha.'

'That pins the bastard down.'

'I still can't see him . . .' Miles stopped, returned to his desk.

'You wouldn't see a twenty-ton lorry slap in front of you,' Dowling remarked.

'I can't believe Harvey was responsible for her murder.'

'Look, sonny boy, when a man has his hands on a woman's throat in the process of raping her and she's so terrified she goes out like a light because of some weird nerve-heart problem, that's murder.'

'It doesn't make sense. Why try to rape her when he'd Helen Gillmore to keep him happy?'

'You think his cows never try to graze the grass on the other side of the fence?'

'I'd swear he's too fond of Helen Gillmore to think of anyone else.'

'You'll learn when you grow up.'

'And if you don't get the news to the skipper this week,' Jenner said, 'we'll be looking at your head hoisted on top of the flagpole.'

Miles made his way along to the next room. Tyler was not there. Miles stared unseeingly at the large scale map of the division which hung on the wall behind the desk as he tried to make sense of his thoughts. It seemed absurd to everyone to imagine one could judge by instinct. Yet his certainty of Harvey's innocence remained. Why?

Tyler hurried into the room, said sarcastically, 'Make yourself at home.' He went round the desk, sat.

'We've just heard from the lab, Sarge. DNA proves the stains on the floor in the office at the farm were from the dead woman. The flesh in the nails was too polluted to say anything.'

Tyler followed Miles out of the room, turned to enter the detective inspector's.

Kirby and Tait waited in No. 1 interview room.

'The forecast's for more rain,' Kirby observed. 'My garden's mud.'

'Are you on clay?'

'Solid yellow clay.'

'Always trouble to cope with, whatever the weather.'

'Impossible.'

They became silent. Social small talk was difficult between two people who possessed nothing in common.

The door was opened by a PC. Harvey and Pascell entered, said curt good mornings, sat on the side of the table which Tait indicated. Tait switched on the tape recorder, announced the date, time and identities of those present.

Kirby said, 'We've asked you to come here to help us clear up certain matters which follow fresh evidence.'

'What is that evidence?' Pascell asked.

'It will soon become clear . . . Mr Harvey, have you previously told us you keep the office in the cowshed locked?'

'Yes.'

'How many keys are there to this lock?'

'There should be three, but I checked and one is missing.'

'Do you know or can you judge when it was lost?'

'No.'

'A question of days, weeks or months?'

'I can't remember.'

'Before the third key was lost, where did you keep the others?'

'One with me, the others with a number of duplicate house keys.'

'You have one on you now?'

'Yes.'

'May I see it, please?'

'What is the reason for this request?' Pascell asked.

'There is a reason for your client not wishing to show it?'

'That does not answer my question.'

'My reason is, I wish to see it.'

Pascell looked as if he was about to repeat what he had just said, but finally nodded at Harvey, who brought a key out of his pocket and passed it across the table.

Kirby visually examined it.

'The reason for your demand?' Pascell persisted.

'Request, not demand. I wished to confirm whether or not it in any way resembled the key found under the dead woman's body.'

'There has been no previous evidence of that.'

'It has not been necessary to refer to it until now.'

'My client should have been informed.'

'He has no such right until any accusation is made.'

'It is a matter of justice.'

'Your client is assured he will receive justice . . . As I have said, Mr Harvey, a similar key with the same model number on its back was found under the body of the woman known as Minnehaha. Clearly, it was dropped before or during the time when she was being lowered into the hole.'

'If you're trying to suggest . . .' Harvey began wildly.

Pascell said quickly, 'Leave suggestions to them.'

'You were very friendly with the dead woman, were you not?' Kirby asked.

'I was friendly.'

'You frequently invited her to your house?'

'Occasionally.'

'Was this when your wife was also at home?'

'My wife disliked Minnehaha.'

'Are you able to say why?'

'Because of her mode of life.'

'Do you think your wife thought her to be promiscuous?'

'Probably.'

'Was the deceased promiscuous?'

'She may have been.'

'You did not try to find out.'

'Certainly not.'

'Have you ever kissed her?'

'A greeting – peck on the cheek, that's all.'

'You never kissed her passionately on the lips?'

'Of course not.'

'Why should that be so unlikely?'

'I'm married.'

'You observe the same discretion with Mrs Gillmore?'

'There is no call for that remark,' Pascell said.

'I withdraw it . . . Mr Harvey, in contradiction to what you have said, you have been observed to kiss the young woman in a passionate manner.'

'When was this supposed occurrence?' Pascell asked.

'Earlier this year.'

'Can you not be more precise?'

'No.'

'You are alleging my client behaved in the manner described, yet cannot say precisely when this was supposed to be? Hardly a sustainable allegation.'

'Mr Harvey, I ask you a second time, did you ever kiss the young woman on her lips?'

'No.'

'Did you ever fondle her breasts while kissing her?'

'No.'

'Did you fondle any other part of her body?'

'No.'

'Were you frequently with her in the office in the cowshed?'

'Only when discussing stock problems or checking milk figures.'

'Did you kiss her in the office?'

'No.'

'When there, did you try to persuade her to have sex?'

'What the hell is this? I liked her except when she was being political, felt sorry for her, respected her skills. That's all.'

'Was she in the office with you at the beginning of the month?'

'I can hardly be expected to remember that.'

Pascell again interrupted. 'Is the date supposed to be of significance? Is it the date on which Minnehaha is presumed to have died?'

'It is within the period in which she died.'

'It would have been equitable first to have explained that.'

Kirby spoke to Harvey. 'When in the office with you, did she have reason to complain you were treating her as if she was a tart?'

'I never gave her the slightest reason to say anything like that.'

'Did she struggle to escape your sexual advances?'

'Can't you understand? It's all nonsense.'

'Was there an occasion when she again objected to your

advances and you feared she was going to scream, so to prevent that because it might attract attention, did you grip her throat to silence her?'

'No!' Harvey shouted.

'To your consternation, did she suddenly collapse and you were forced to accept she had died?'

'I didn't ever try to make love to her, I did not ever touch her sexually, I did not ever try to rape her,' Harvey said hoarsely.

'We have evidence to the contrary.'

'Detail that evidence,' Pascell said.

'Someone saw your client enter the milk shed with the young woman. He heard the sounds of struggle in the office and her verbal attempts to prevent your client having unwelcome sex with her.'

'The name of your witness?'

'Wade made certain allegations before it became known the woman was dead. His testimony, therefore, bears the ring of truth.'

'It was as the result of this evidence that my client became a suspect?'

'It contributed to our considering whether your client would be able to help us in our investigation.'

'Have you ignored the certainty that Wade was lying.'

'No.'

'Yet have uncovered no reason to doubt what he says?'

'No.'

Pascell spoke in a very low voice to Harvey before addressing Kirby once more. 'My client denies absolutely, without equivocation, that there is the slightest truth in the allegations you have made.'

'Mr Harvey, when alive, did the young woman wear a bracelet?'

'Yes.'

'Did you suggest to her it might be unwise to wear this when in the commune?'

'Yes.'

'Are you aware the bracelet was not found on her body?'

'No.'

'Can you suggest where it might now be?'

'No.'

Kirby looked at Tait, who shook his head, said, 'There are no more questions for the moment.'

Tait detailed the time the interview ended, switched off the recorder. He extracted two tapes, signed them, handed one to Pascell.

'Well?' asked Kirby when the other two had left.

'You didn't think it was time to charge and arrest him?' Tait asked.

'You are prepared to accept Wade's evidence without examining that very closely?'

'As you pointed out, sir, Wade indicated Harvey's amorous intentions before the girl was known to be dead.'

'Which makes for presumptive evidence, not proof.'

'Add it to all the other evidence . . .'

'And you are in danger of making as big a mistake as when you claimed Mrs Harvey was dead,' Kirby said, as he replaced papers in their folder. 'Make out an enlarged file and send it to me. After I've cleared it, it can go to the CPS for them to decide whether to bring a case. Have a description of the missing bracelet sent to all the usual sources.'

'You imagine the murderer could be stupid enough to risk trying to sell it?'

'Murderers aren't sensible. Harvey is in need of money.'

'It doesn't sound to be worth nearly enough to help him.'

'He'll be optimistic. And perhaps it has an antique value on top of its intrinsic one.'

Helen met Harvey in the hall. 'What on earth was it this time?'

'The question you thought they could never be stupid enough to ask. Had I attempted to rape Minnehaha and had she died suddenly when I tried to stop her screaming?'

'Oh God!' she murmured. She gripped him tightly.

TWENTY-THREE

Miles stepped into Tyler's room. 'Sarge, I couldn't sleep last night . . .'

'You think I'm the department's agony aunt?'

'I started thinking about Mr Harvey and the first time I questioned Wade because it was thought Mrs Harvey was missing. When I said who I was, he looked as if he'd been belted in the stomach.'

'Meeting you can have that effect.'

'At the time, I thought he'd probably been worried we'd found out he'd been poaching or helping himself elsewhere, but last night I got to realizing that would never have scared him, because being a countryman, he'd never be caught poaching or lifting the odd bit of wood. And I wondered why he'd been so quick to tell me about Harvey chasing Minnehaha. What if, as Mr Harvey keeps saying, that was all lies? Why would Wade lie? To suggest a motive for murder if ever Minnehaha's body was found?'

'Suppose you try to explain what you're saying?'

'Wade murdered her, not Mr Harvey. It wasn't just surprise at hearing I was a copper, he was terrified. Why? He must have known Minnehaha was dead. He thought her body had been found and we knew he was the murderer.'

'Anything more?'

'That's it.'

'Then I suggest you go along to the guv'nor and tell him that he and the DCS have been making fools of themselves.'

'You don't think there's anything in what I've said?'

'That it's a whole lot of what one doesn't name in polite society.'

In November, the first light fall of snow dusted the countryside as far south as Berkshire; a wind from the east brought icy roads and traffic confusion.

Miles, the only member of CID present, ignored the computer on which he was working and stared into space. Where to have their honeymoon? Corfu, Sardinia, Turkey? Irene often talked about the West Indies and the blue skies, warm sea, daiquiris, coconut palms. He wasn't certain about the coconuts. To go there would fulfil her dreams. But, as he was learning, marriage would double expenses . . .

The phone rang, returning him to the CID general room.

'Swaine here, Monkton and Sons, Bleambury. Some time ago, you asked for information regarding a bracelet. From the description you gave, that bracelet may have been offered to us. Our attention was first drawn because the customer was not dressed as are our usual ones. Of course, these days dress is unfortunately often a guide to financial, not social standing . . . I digress. Your description was not detailed enough for me to be certain that this was the bracelet I was being shown, but since it was made of gold and undoubtedly of Roman origin, I was reasonably confident it might well be. I valued it at two thousand pounds. The man tried to increase my offer, said he would think about it and left.'

'Did you recognize him?'

'No.'

'You hadn't seen his photo in the papers or on the telly recently?'

'I think not.'

Surely, he would have recognized Harvey after all the publicity concerning the "missing wife"? 'Thanks very much, Mr Swaine. We'll be getting back on to you.'

Miles replaced the receiver, hurried through to Tyler's room. 'I was right, sarge.'

Tyler crossed out half a line on a printed report. 'A unique event.'

'I've just received a phone call.'

'If it's not too much trouble, explain what you're trying to tell me.'

'Swaine, a jeweller in Bleambury, has phoned to say a man was in his shop offering a Roman gold bracelet. He can't swear to it, but is pretty certain it was the bracelet described in the notice we sent out. I asked him if he recognized the man. He didn't, which means it wasn't Harvey.'

'With that kind of logic, you believe the earth is flat.'

'He'll have seen Harvey's photo on the telly and in the papers time and again.'

'How long ago did that happen?'

'I don't know. Six, seven weeks.'

'Five months. Do you remember images of faces from that long ago?'

'The man was badly dressed and Swaine obviously didn't think it likely he could legitimately own an antique bracelet worth a couple of thousand quid.'

'It has not occurred to you that Harvey does not milk cows and shovel dung in his best bib and tucker?'

'But he'd never go to an upmarket jewellers in his working clothes.'

'How do you know they're upmarket?'

'The man who phoned sounded very superior.'

'Jewellers fake their voices like some of the jewellery they sell.'

'It could well have been Wade.'

'It could have been the Chancellor of the Exchequer, who's very short of cash.'

'We've got to fax Mr Swain a photo of Mr Harvey.'

'Giving orders again?'

'When I told Wade I was CID . . .'

'Don't give me that crap again.'

'You don't think I'm right?'

'You catch on quickly.'

'Is it OK if I fax a photo then?'

'In your own time. And you'll pay for the fax.'

Miles returned to the general room. How to get hold of a photo of Harvey? He remembered the reporter from one of the local papers was always willing to help if in return he was occasionally provided with information. Photos would be filed in the paper's morgue. And come to that, there was also the possibility Wade had been photographed. Anyone who was obviously connected with events of a news value usually was.

* * *

Dowling was explaining to the bored Miles and Jenner the incompetence of the English rugby team who had lost heavily the previous Saturday. The phone rang, Jenner answered, then called out, 'Eric.'

Miles crossed to the desk, picked up the receiver.

'Swaine here. I've studied the two photos you faxed me. Number two is the man who brought the bracelet in question to my shop.'

As Miles replaced the receiver, Dowling paused in his criticism of the fly half who had dropped so many passes, his hands must have been coated in grease. 'Was that anything to upset the calm?'

'I scored a try.'

'You wouldn't know what a rugger pitch looks like.'

'Which is why I don't have a broken nose and missing front teeth.' Miles made his way to the next room.

Tyler ignored him for a while, finally looked up. 'You've come to explain why the world is flat?'

'I've just had Swaine on the phone, Sarge.'

'Don't bother to tell me who he is.'

'The jeweller in Bleambury who reported that a man wanted to sell the bracelet that was probably Minnehaha's. I sent him photos and he's named the customer.'

'Harvey. Making nonsense of your theories.'

'Wade.'

'You're talking straight?'

'As an arrow.'

Tyler stared at Miles as he slowly accepted the consequences of what he had been told.

'I was right after all and the rest of you were wrong!'

'A word of wisdom. Tell a senior who doesn't have my generous nature that he's wrong with such obvious pleasure and he'll look for you every time there's a dirty job to be done.'

Miles left. He had proved himself a detective, Tyler thought, and his work folder would have in it, "Recommended for CID", signed DS Tyler.

Tait was on the phone and Tyler waited, appearing to be disinterested in what was being said while listening closely.

'They think we're bloody magicians . . . If it's not priority, it can wait,' Tait said as he replaced the receiver.

'Sir, a jeweller in Bleambury has been offered a bracelet by a badly dressed man. The bracelet seemed to match Minnehaha's.'

'Was it hers?'

'He can't be absolutely certain and the customer refused the offer and took the bracelet away with him.'

'Will the jeweller be able to identify the man?'

'Young Eric, whose initiative it was to check, has gained a positive identification.'

'Harvey.'

'No, Sir.'

'Then either the identification of the ring or of the man is nonsense.'

'Not necessarily. After all, we have always accepted the possibility that the guilty man might not be Harvey.'

'And?' Tait asked sharply.

'Two photographs were sent to Swaine. He identified Wade.'

After a while, Tait said. 'I can't say I'm surprised.'

'No, sir.' Tyler would have been surprised if Tait had admitted he was surprised.

'I will tell Chief Superintendent Kirby that we are now certain our reservations were justified. Wade, not Harvey, is guilty of the murder. And perhaps I might tactfully point out to him that facts can sometimes offer ambiguous conclusions, just as assumptions can.'

Harvey drove too quickly and had to brake sharply, which scattered the gravel. He had just stepped out of the car when Helen opened the front door.

'What's happened?' she called out, her voice high because of fear.

He walked across. 'There was a phone call on my mobile, asking me to go and see the police.'

'Why didn't you tell me? Oh, God, they aren't going to . . .'

'Mr Tait thought it right they should tell me personally that I was no longer a suspect in the murder of Minnehaha.'

'You mean . . . It's over . . . I needn't have the nightmare of thinking . . .' She put her arms around him, pressed herself against him. Tears of relief and happiness slid down her cheeks.

Later, in the sitting room, she asked, 'What happens now?'

'I will be called as a witness and that will be the end of it.'

'What about us? You, Gillian, me?'

'She's told me that the rows, accusations, questions, rumours, have upset her so much, she's decided she will divorce me and live with Fiona in Australia.'

'Oh! . . . D'you think maybe she and Fiona . . .' She stopped.

He shrugged his shoulders.

'What about the farm?'

'She will give me an agricultural tenancy which provides her with further income. This means I won't have owner-ship, but will have guaranteed occupation. So when the dust has settled we can marry and, to Mrs Spens' great relief, our immoral relationship will come to an end.'

'But, hopefully, not the immorality,' she murmured before she kissed him.